exodus of
angels

exodus of angels

ellen curtis
matthew ledrew

Published in Canada by Engen Books, St. John's, NL.

Library and Archives Canada Cataloguing in Publication
Curtis, Ellen, 1993-. Author
       Exodus of angels / Ellen Curtis, Matthew LeDrew.
ISBN 978-1-926903-28-6 (paperback)
       I. LeDrew, Matthew, 1984-, author II. Title.
PS8605.U78E86 2016   C813'.6   C2016-900911-4

Distributed by:
Engen Books
www.engenbooks.com
submissions@engenbooks.com

First mass market paperback printing: April 2016

Cover Image: Ellen Curtis

To our friend
Matthew Daniels
and for Maya Reilly.

PROLOGUE

Los Angeles, California

November 10th

The sound of heavy footfalls on concrete echoed in her ears. She could smell the dank smoke that lingered in the air in the alleys, and the garbage piling along the sides of old brick buildings. Her breath was tight in her lungs and she braced herself with her hands on her knees, gasping for breath.

The sound of sirens grew closer.

With a stitch below her right rib, she pushed off from the wall and rounded the corner. The streets were packed, making it easy enough for her to just become another face in the crowd. She walked slowly, hand on her side and breath returning to her lungs. Her heartbeat slowed to a more normal tempo, and she felt herself relax.

Then she heard the shouting. She felt her heart catch in her throat.

Her head shot up and she whipped around, taking in her surroundings. Tall buildings loomed overhead and lined the street with offices for large corporations, none of which would be a good place to duck into and hide in. Her eyes met those of a man slowly pushing a cart along the side of the street. He had a hollow look to his face that struck at something in her, and she found herself mesmerized just staring at him. Something about him seemed familiar to her, and she moved toward him, forgetting where she was.

In her daze, she stumbled and crashed into a tall man. The force of the collision snapped her out of the trance, only for her to discover that she and the stranger had become covered in coffee. He stared angrily at his shirt, mouth agape and on the brink of yelling at her. She didn't give him the chance to, hastily backing away from him and pushing forward.

She sped up her pace, weaving through the crowd. If she remembered correctly, a metro stop was just around the corner. If she could get there, she could go anywhere. She took a deep breath.

The yelling behind her was getting louder.

She glanced over her shoulder and saw two officers pushing through the crowd; it looked like one was waving a photograph. They were only a few feet from the man whom she had banged into, and she could see he was moving through the crowd toward them.

She broke into a full run. The corner was only a short distance away. She had a small opportunity for escape, and it hinged on being able to make it to the subway before she could be detained.

She swerved through the crowd, the yelling behind her buzzing in her ears. All the sounds of the street assailed her as she sprinted toward her goal. Her feet ached and she felt a spasm in the sole of her foot. She pushed on through the pain and turned the corner. The metro was less than twenty feet in front of her. She paused only briefly to catch her breath, then darted forward through the crowd.

She barely made it two feet before a hand grabbed her arm and forced her to the ground.

She felt a sharp prick in the side of her neck. Pressed onto the concrete, she became aware of the chill on her legs. The oversized trench coat she had fastened around her hospital gown was filthy and did little to mitigate the bite of autumn air. It suddenly dawned on her that the thin socks on her feet hadn't protected her from the shards of glass littering the street. In that brief moment of clarity, she wondered how she had even made it this far. She had no recollection of why she had started running, or what she had been running from, just that it was far removed from the city she had grown up in, the one she had been running through.

She felt a sob catch in her throat as she felt her mind slipping away.

Her body went limp, and the man kneeling over her relaxed his grip on her arms. He stood, capping the needle he had injected into her neck seconds before. The two police officers were clearing the crowd around him, but above the ruckus he could hear the wailing of an ambulance siren. It came into view after only a few moments, and when it did two paramedics bolted out, retrieving a stretcher from the back. From the cab of the vehicle, a young, distinguished looking woman emerged. As the paramedics placed the girl on the stretcher, she walked over to greet him.

"The situation is contained, I take it?" she asked, her even tone only broken by the small sneer that crept in at the end of her sentence.

The man glared. "Of course it is. Just another basket case off her meds that the police had to apprehend for her own safety. Nothing that will show up on the evening news. No reason for you to be here."

The woman smiled coldly at him. "That's precisely why you're hired as lab assistant and I'm in charge of public relations, Mr. Harrison. Kindly escort Miss Loveless back to Black Springs while I deal with the police and the press."

"What press are you referring to exactly?" Harrison asked, but as he glanced around, he understood his question was already answered.

"The ones who are going to want to know why the daughter of a Fortune 500 CEO is running around downtown in a dressing gown. Mr. Loveless pays for our discretion, Harrison. Now he's going to want us to pay for this. Play your cards right and you might not be the one to pay."

With that, Sylvia Aaron turned and walked away from him, moving forward to address the crowd of reporters that had gathered just beyond the police. Her heels clicked sharply on the sidewalk and as Harrison turned away from her, he cast a bitter look in her direction.

Alice Loveless was becoming a bigger headache for Black Springs Clinic than he had ever imagined.

CHAPTER 01

November 15th

Leigh lay with her head against Theo's chest, the flickering light from the TV illuminating their features in a shadowy blue wash. The Styrofoam takeout containers on the coffee table in front of them still held stray bits of noodle and sauce, and in the quiet moments of the muted commercial break she could hear the gurgles of Theo's stomach digesting the food. The sheer normalcy of it was bliss for her. She snuggled into him tightly, and she felt the comforting weight of his hand rest on her head.

"Would you rather go to bed soon?" Theo asked. "We can turn this off anytime."

"No, I'm good here," she replied. "I want to know if the guy ends up getting away with murder or not."

Theo smiled down at her. She had seemed more and more sick lately -- angrier too -- but the second they were watching true crime documentaries, the rest of the world seemed to melt away. She became Leigh free of the scary past and future, and free of fear; instead she had a belly full of takeout and a semi-serious addiction to dramatized murder investigations. He wished he could freeze the moment; that they could just stay here like this forever.

Then the door buzzed.

Leigh sighed, knocking Theo's hand off her head as she sat up. "I thought no one was supposed to be able to get into your building unless they had a key or were buzzed in from the ground."

Theo rose, brow creasing. "Yeah, they're not."

He left the living room and made his way down the hall to the door, grabbing a sword off the display on the wall as he went. He held it by his side, muscle memory itching to be called upon if needed.

The thick must of cigar smoke crept under the door, causing Theo's stomach to churn. He neared the entryway cautiously, inching forward to peer through the peephole. He sighed when he saw who lay beyond, resting the sword behind the door before opening it.

"Mr. Flaherty, I have an offer if you are ready."

The man's tall frame blocked most of the light from the hall, but Theo still blinked against the brightness. Theo motioned for him to come in and managed to grunt out something about turning on the light. The man obliged and, as his eyes adjusted to the light, Theo found himself cursing inwardly.

The man was Clive Federico, and Theo was used to only seeing him when his father wanted to pass along bad news. In the days leading up to Black Springs, Clive had been an almost constant presence in Theo's life, micromanaging Theo's life to suit his father's. He had hoped to skirt by under the radar in the L.A. apartment; however Clive's presence only proved his naïveté.

Clive's tightly gelled hair was mussed, a few strands hanging above his brow. A thick cigar clung between his lips, though it had been smoked away to close to nothing. His suit showed signs of creasing, the crispness fading from it as he smoked and followed Theo back toward the living room. Theo didn't anticipate much good coming out of the little time left in the night.

Leigh stiffened as she saw Theo return flanked by the broad smoking man, and her eyes darted about in a way that Theo recognized meant she was searching for the closest weapon. He sighed. "Clive, Leigh. Leigh, Clive," he said, motioning lazily between the two. "My least favourite evil henchman."

Clive scowled at Theo's sarcasm, then turned to Leigh and smiled. "Good to finally meet you, Ms. Blackheart."

Theo's eyes lowered as Leigh nodded back respectfully.

"I've spoken to your father, Theo," Clive continued, his tone changing from conversational to a lower octave used for business. "He was surprised to hear you're doing so... well. I can't say he's terribly surprised about the company you're keeping though."

Theo did not respond to the prod, but smiled in Leigh's direction.

"Theodore," Clive continued, his tone shifting again to one of condescension as smoke curled around his head and he took another draw. "Your father has decided to be generous. The lease his accountants have maintained on this apartment was never meant to extend beyond your admission a few years ago. Understandably, he's not too happy about that touchy little time in your father-son history, but he's willing to let it all slide if you follow his... conditions," he finished with a smirk.

"That didn't suit me so well last time he tried to be generous," Theo mumbled.

Clive smiled, though the smile was cold and twisted and caused a shiver to dance along the hairs on Theo's arms. "His offer is for thirty million dollars, deposited into your bank account upon your agreement to leave Los Angeles by the end of the week. He wants you to take your girlfriend with you, and he never wants to see either of your names in the news again. He never wants to hear from you again. His public image is too important for you to tarnish with all of these upsets." Each sentence was punctuated by puff on his cigar, filling the room with a hazy cloud.

"Gladly, on the condition that for the next week he won't interfere while I tie up any loose ends I have with people here," Theo replied, allowing himself to finally relax, even if only marginally.

Clive paid little attention to Theo, turning his cigar over in his hand and examining it before glancing out the window at the streets below. "Theodore, I wouldn't test your father's patience. Paying one last visit to the buxom brunette you dated in high school certainly won't make him rescind his offer, but going after old rivals and asking too many questions just might."

Leigh's eyebrows furrowed, and her lips pursed. She bristled the longer Clive remained in their home, his presence an almost tangible poison in their sleepy evening.

Theo's lip formed an involuntary grimace, though he never noticed Leigh's discomfort. "I know my father and his deals. Either way, by the week's end Leigh and I will be gone. We just need to figure out what works for us."

The man in the suit crossed the floor, pressing the tip of his cigar against the bare flesh of Theo's arm as he spoke, leaning in to whisper in Theo's ear. "I sincerely hope, for your sake, your needs match up with your father's. He has far worse things in his arsenal than locking you away and pumping you full of medication and despair."

Fire flared in Leigh's eyes, but she bit her tongue, watching Theo's reaction for some cue as to what she should do.

Theo didn't flinch. He had his own arsenal. He had his own mission.

CHAPTER 02

September 8th

The tent was hot, packed with people so tight that they pressed against each other in cheap, plastic folding chairs. There was an old black woman in the front row wearing a flower-print dress and waving a laminate programme at herself that did little to quell the trails of sweat that dribbled down her neck and into her blouse.

The white fabric of the tent seemed to breathe with the people within it, pushing out and then sucking back in between each support beam. It had started a crisp, clean white, but was faded into eggshell in places and brown in others; life on the road had reached into it and changed it. There was a large stain by the west corner from where a hand had left a large tin of instant coffee atop it in the back of the truck and it had rained heavily on the way back from a New Jersey show.

Caleb Galen stood at the center of the stage. From here, the heat that came from every person in the room was a wave that crashed down on him with every exhalation, the stomps of their feet and the claps of their hands like jungle drums. He could feel their reverberations in the center of his chest, pumping and beating its way throughout him. He spread his arms and the crowd picked up their tempo, all the different shoes and sandals somehow creating one unified sound.

The tent always faced the East. That had been a stipulation from the very beginning. Magnetic East was not good enough – true East had to be attained. Before every show the difference between magnetic north and true north was Googled and calculated until finally the opening flap to the tent faced true east.

There was a young woman in the front row with blonde hair and bright green eyes. She wore a white blouse, had red lips, and fanned herself lightly with a folding fan. Sweat dotted her brow along the line where her hair had been pulled back. Her eyes locked with his and his with hers for a long moment. Caleb smiled. So did she. When she did, she hid herself behind the fan and looked away, but it was not long before her eyes found their way back. His dark hair was slicked back and was thick with the heat of the room. He wore a white suit with a black shirt underneath that had no collar or tie. He'd always been insistent on that: no collars. His skin was clear and his cheekbones high and when he smiled he smiled with his entire face. He was seventeen, but looked twenty. She was twenty, but looked seventeen.

He laughed heartily and threw his head back; nobody in the crowd seemed to question why. They clapped their hands, stomped their feet, and fanned their fans. The fans did little, but the clapping and the stomping had the effect of drinking cool absinth on a long day in the summer sun.

"Can you feel it?" he called out, looking at the light that hung from the ceiling before his gaze shifted back down to the crowd. He tried to make eye contact with all of them and none of them, to have the effect of one of those paintings that seemed to follow you with its eyes.

There were positive hoots and hollers from the crowd as the stomping died down all on its own, the clapping stopping as soon as the question was poised.

He walked to the other side of the stage and took his microphone from its stand. "Can you feel the power of the energy in this room? That's your power! That's the power that you bring here with you, that you have inside of you every day! So I'll ask you again: can you feel it?"

There was a resounded outcry of YES from the crowd, so loud that even the heavy fabric of the tent couldn't dampen it.

"The power of faith exists in all things, in every part of you. Faith isn't something that can be kept in a church or a book or a tent. Faith is bigger than us; faith is all of us. Faith is us working together for what we want until we are something bigger than ourselves."

He pointed to a middle-aged man in the middle row with a gaunt face and a uniform on. He looked too old to be wearing the uniform he was, as though he'd seen war late in life. "They say that without faith there wouldn't be war, but they don't understand what faith is! Faith is the power to believe, and to use that belief to change the world around you! And there are going to be those who use that power for ill, but we can use that power – here! Tonight! – to do something better! Do you believe with me?"

There was another yes, the force of it coming with a blast of heat that might have knocked his hair back.

Caleb looked down, his eyes scanning the crowd until they fell upon a woman in her mid-forties with saggy cheeks but firm breasts. "Margaret?" he called to her, raising his hand up. She nodded and got to her feet. She was clutching her right hand with her left. He motioned to his own. "What happened, Margaret?"

She looked down at her hand. It was shaped normally, but the color was wrong – green and dusky in some places and pale in others. She held it up, displayed by her good hand, as though the sight of it were explanation in and of itself. He smiled at her leadingly, and after a moment she spoke. "There was a forklift at work – the brakes went and it rolled. I couldn't get out of the way. I can't work and I can't play."

"Piano?" Caleb asked.

She nodded.

He waved her toward the front. As she shuffled her way painfully past other patrons, he turned to the rest of those amassed. "Margaret needs us, friends. This is why we're here today. Despite what you think, nobody comes to the tent because they believe – they come because they want to believe. If your arm is broken, do not come here; go to the doctors and the nurses. But if your faith is broken, come here and be restored! Margaret needs you now, everyone. She needs you to prove what faith can do and what faith can be! Can you do it?"

Yes.

"Let me be the instrument of your love for Margaret!

Let me feel your faith pass through me and into her! I have faith, in all of you! You can do this, we can do this, together!"

Margaret had made her way up to Caleb and now stood on the floor directly before him. He reached out his hand to pull her up, then thought better of it, and stepped down to join her. He reached out to touch her hand and she pulled it away, even that motion causing her visible agony.

"It's okay," he smiled, his dark eyes penetrating her. "In faith, all things are possible."

She gave him her hand and he cupped both of his around it. She winced once, then relented, her shoulders loosening.

"I need everyone's help, I can't do this alone!" he yelled, smiling.

The crowd began to stomp and clap again. The old black lady with the fan began to hum an old southern hymn.

He left his left hand fall away, holding onto her right tightly with his own. He brought his head down and pressed his lips into the gap between his thumb and forefinger, his cheeks puffed with air until he let it all out. His face was bright and aglow with sweat, and Margaret could see his every pore. With his eyes closed he looked different, shadier somehow, like someone who would sell you a bad used car in a decade's time. The light on his face became brighter and brighter, and the room became hot – unbearably hot, as though someone had turned up the thermostat on the world. Which someone had, if Al Gore was to be believed.

The glow ebbed away and the heat subsided until it was back to its normal level of unbearableness. He stood back up and straightened his shirt and then took his hand away from hers.

The color had returned, pink and full and peachy throughout. The knuckles were smooth now, no longer swollen and tender as they had been even before the accident. The skin had been pulled tight and smooth, and the veins were now nestled calmly beneath the surface of the skin.

Margaret brought her hand up in front of her face and wriggled her fingers, ready to recoil from the burn of it, but feeling only the thickness of the air in the tent as it passed between her fingers. She smiled at first, and then broke down into ecstatic tears.

Caleb placed a hand on her shoulder. "You'll have to play me something, the next time we're in town," he said.

She laughed and smiled and nodded and cried all at once. She seemed as though she were going to hug him, but he led her by her shoulder back to the lane to her seat. There was applause.

"I need you to understand," he continued, addressing the crowd. "That wasn't me; that was you. You had the power to do that all along. Through the power of your faith, Margaret can enjoy her life again. Quality in life is something we all deserve, and that quality can only come from faith! Do you hear me?"

Yes. There was clapping again, and cheering.

The blonde girl with the green eyes smiled at him again. He nodded to her, then turned his attention to a man in the back. The left side of his face sagged and did not respond with the rest of it, and his one arm lay impotently at his side. "Craig?" he called.

The man nodded and hobbled forward a step.

"Will you be the next one to let your community help you?" he asked, taking a step back. The crowd all moved to the left suddenly; without moving their seats or their feet, they shifted. He stopped, shook his head, then found Craig in his new position just to the left. "Would you give us that? Would you let us prove our faith and strengthen our faith with you?"

The clapping and the stomping stopped. He blinked twice and he wasn't looking at the crowd anymore; they all dropped away as though the tent had been erected not just facing east but also atop a large trap door. The ceiling came into view suddenly, the whole tent having been tilted on its side. It took him a moment to realize that he was on his back. He'd fallen backward and smashed his head against the stage he'd been on a moment ago. He heard the sound from it now almost a full twenty seconds late, like watching someone chop wood in the distance and the sound didn't reach until the man's arms were back in the air again.

He tried to get up, but threw up immediately. It was hard to breathe; he could take a breath, but it was like his chest refused to expand to accommodate the extra air. He laid his head back down and stared up at the ceiling with milky eyes. After a moment, his mother was looking down at him. He could see that she was clutching his cheeks between her thumb and forefinger, but could not see it. Behind her shoulder, the blonde girl looked on, her face twisted in worry and disgust. His mother was saying something, but sound had gone away and all that was left was the hazy, foggy reality of the tent, like a silent film.

In the west, the sun was setting.

CHAPTER 03

Stanford University

November 15th

The chalk scraped across the teal green chalkboard, making a scratching sound that could be heard at the very back of the lecture hall. Large flakes of white spewed from its tip in every direction as it pressed too tight against the chalkboard.

The hand that held it was ashen gray with large thick, cracked nails.

He finished carving out the N in Darwin with a cascade of white creamy smoke, then stepped back a pace to examine his work. There were six names on the board divided into two columns of three. Marx, Tylor, and Morgan were on the left and Spencer, Freud and Darwin were on the right. The names on the right were slightly bigger than the names on the left, the tails of each consonant loopier and more feminine.

Jona turned back to his class. Just under fifty students stared back at him and at the board behind him with faces that ranged from interested to vacant to hot with the mad scribble to write down what was on the board exactly the way he had written it. Some even seemed to be trying to copy his handwriting, just in case a loopy N had something to do with the point he was trying to make. Several just watched him.

He was a large man of almost seven feet in height. His shoulders were far across and bulged against his shirt at the ends. He was bald, with a faintest hint of light stubble around his ears, and there were small round ridges in his forehead beneath his skin. They started just above his eyebrows and went all the way to the back of his head, spaced evenly until they met in a single point on the back of his head. His skin was that same dark, ashen gray all over, dry and flakey in the crooks of his arms and below each small eye. The chalk was tiny between his massive, plump fingers.

"We've been studying the six of these people for the last three classes," he said, rapping the board with a large, swollen knuckle. "Assuming you've been doing the readings and taking notes, can anyone tell me what they have in common?"

The class's gaze shifted, as one, from Jona to the six names listed on the board. There was a young man with slick red hair in the second row that looked as though he wanted to open his mouth and speak. Jona smiled and nodded at him to encourage it, but he said nothing. After a moment, he shook his head and scribbled something into the margin of his notebook.

Jona turned and drew a large circle around the six scholars, then laid the chalk down on the ridge of the board. "We're studying classical theory here. What do these six have in common?"

A girl with brunette hair and a sweater with a Greek letter on it spoke up from the back row. "None of them are anthropologists?"

"None of them are anthropologists," Jona nodded. He tapped the board again. "Then why do we study them? Ahh, that's a good one, hey? I bet they wouldn't let me teach this course if I just picked whatever I wanted. It'd have to have something to do with anthropology, so what is it? Freud was a psychoanalyst. What's he doing on the list?" He paused. "They all influenced anthropological thinking. Classical anthropology is full of these writers that weren't anthropologists; writers that we've..."

"Stolen?"

"... Adopted, over the years." He smiled in the general direction of where the voice had come from. "That's why Anne Frank's diary is considered an anthropological text. She didn't set to write an ethnography, but in the end that's what a diary is – just most of the time what's in your diary won't be particularly relevant to the data on your culture."

There were a few laughs. He turned and looked back at the class, smiling. It hadn't been funny, and he knew that.

"So we know why Miss Frank was adopted in; why were these six? There must be a reason."

"They influenced anthropological thinking," said Tessa, a bigger girl from the middle row and one of the few he knew the name of.

"How?"

She looked at the six names on the board. "They were

writing on society."

"They were writing on society," Jona nodded, smiling broadly. "Each of them had their own ideas about what made society work and tick. Society and its Discontents, it's right there in the title. Now each of them were a little right and a little... not right. But each of them, even when they were wrong, sparked the beginnings of anthropological thought. Freud was ethnocentric because he assumed the nuclear family relationships he saw in the western world were universal, and they aren't. Things are different. Things change." He drew a line from the edge of the circle and wrote the word Society.

"There's that important question: what things are socially generated? Freud says we created society to make us happy, and yet now all it does is make us unhappy. So why do we keep it? Why is it kept everywhere, in various forms?"

Several students had shifted their gaze away from him. He followed their gaze to the door, where a tall man with long blonde hair and a well-kept beard stood squarely. His jaw was set tight and his black tee clung to his frame as though it were afraid to let go.

Jona nodded at him and smiled, then turned back to the class. "We began to think – and to realize – that everything was created. That the social norms that we thought of as universal to humanity were not hard-grained into our DNA, but were instead a part of our social constraints and constructions. Prohibitions against incest are socially generated. Prohibitions against murder are socially generated. God is socially generated. Animalism is socially generated. Pottery is socially generated. And so on and so on, and you get the idea."

He turned back to the doorway. The man with the long hair was gone.

"Law, art, moral rules... all these things are socially generated, and all come from this central, burning question: where did we come from?" He paused and looked at his watch, which he kept off his wrist and propped up on his desk by its own strap. "That'll be all for today. Remember for next class, read Durkheim's essay on Religious Life and Weber's essay on Charismatic Authority. Ronnie and Claire, you'll both owe me commentaries."

The students started packing up their things and made their way out. Jona stood and watched them go until there were none left, then turned to the board and erased it until there was no trace of the names left.

The cafeteria was large and open. There was a half faux-wall made of brick and glass dividing the kitchen and the line to it from the rest of the seating area. Jona could see the man with the blonde hair through it from the moment he stepped in, sitting comfortably at the far end of the hall. There was a tiny cup of espresso in front of him sending steam wafting up into his chin and beard, and a small plate next to it that held half of a fluffy, buttery croissant. He was looking out into the crowd of students between he and Jona, studying each face, even the ones that were turned away from him, with something resembling fascination until he came to some stark realization and then moved on to the next. He moved from one to the next in a linear fashion, until arriving naturally on Jona.

He held on him for a long moment, then motioned to the seat across from him.

Jona made his way across the hall, dodging students as they moved past with their faces down in cell phones and laptops. He was large, and had to stop abruptly once so that a girl carrying a tray with an omelette on it did not lose it. The blonde man watched him the entire way, never once breaking eye contract, following him like a camera on a track until he stood next to that table.

"Victor," Jona said, his voice heavy and raspy.

Victor nodded and motioned again to the chair. Jona sat down. They regarded each other for several long moments. Students continued to walk past. Eventually Victor let his eyes fall away and back out into the crowd, eventually settling on a plump girl with curly black hair sitting against the window with a ham sandwich and an off-brand soda-pop. She glanced over in their general direction several times, but always moved her eyes back to her laptop.

"She likes you," Victor said, taking a small sip of his espresso.

"Who?"

"The girl by the window. Brunette, bigger."

Jona looked. "Tessa? She's a child."

"Well I wasn't suggesting you go over and ask her to fellate you. I was only saying."

Jona watched her for a moment until she looked up at him, blushed, then quickly turned back to her laptop. He frowned and shook his head, then turned back to Victor. "To what do I owe the pleasure?"

"I was in the area, thought I would drop in and say

hello." There was a long pause. "I enjoyed the lecture, what little I heard of it." Another pause. "Do you think you'll get to Mary Douglas?"

A woman came over a laid a deep, hot cup of tea down in front of Jona. He hadn't ordered and did not have to; he had the same thing every time. He took a sip while it was still steaming and did not seem to notice the heat. "It's classical theory. We start with Marx and end with Wolf. No room for Douglas."

Victor nodded.

"That's the thing about this field, we're always teaching westerners not to think like westerners. I don't think it'll ever change. Math and history and economics... all these things we teach young people younger and younger; we have to update the curriculum once they hit post secondary. Not anthropology. No matter how many years I teach this, they're always surprised when they learn the things they take for granted as human behavior are just learned behavior. That it's just... social. And then, that society can change. That it has changed, that it will change – well, not what their high school teachers prepared them for, let me tell you."

Victor winced. "I'm heading into Los Angeles."

"I always thought you could use some color."

"I was hoping to avoid any trouble once I got there."

Jona clacked his tongue against the roof of his mouth. Even it was discolored, slightly. He took a sip from his tea. In his large hands, even his deep mug looked like an espresso cup. It looked silly and dainty for a man of his size to be drinking it in such small, careful sips. "I did some research in Korea recently. South of course, I'm not insane."

"I didn't even realize you were back in the field."

"Well, I can't stay an armchair anthropologist forever. You've got to get to where the blood is, as they say. Anyway, I was there trying to get a sense of war mentality, how it's changed, especially since Viet Nam. I mean, say what you want about Iraq or Afghanistan, but South Korea has some real problems. Anyway, I was explaining my research and findings to a few first years in my intro class earlier this semester, and they could not fathom that there would ever be a time when Korea was not divided. When the world did not think in terms of North and South."

Victor smiled.

"Amazing, isn't it? It made me feel old. I reminded them that we thought the same of East and West Germany. And about the USSR. Most of them had no clue what I was referring to."

"And these are anthropology students? Good luck with that."

"They're young. But it shows you, doesn't it? Just how far we've come. From the issue dominating our thoughts to it being a footnote in history. Things always balance, things always reach a point of cohesion."

Victor nodded. "I suppose they do."

"Do you know what Tyler called the things that lasted from one part of a cultural evolution to the next, Prophet? He called them a survival. Such a good word for it, don't you think?"

Victor finished his coffee and moved his croissant to the edge of the table, away from himself.

"All things have to change at some point. All things

shift. Even a society as big and as rich as this one. The change is happening, protests, all that – it lacks cohesion. The government learned too much in the sixties, but soon things will be big enough to move forward. Soon we will have hegemony and agency, and we will act – and there will be change." He leaned in as much as he could with his massive frame. "When that happens, I'll be fine with being the product of a bygone age. What about you? Do you hope to be a survival?"

Victor leveled his gaze. "As I understand it, there were holes in Tyler's work. Too many survivals."

"It's called theory."

Victor leaned back on his chair. "If you push it, I'll push back. Dirt may be matter out of place, but you can call me a broom."

Jona sighed, put his mug aside, then rose to his feet. "It was nice seeing you again, as always... give my love to Natasha."

Victor narrowed his eyes. "You're scared of the windmills."

Jona stopped.

"You've started them turning, like a gust of warm summer air. And that's what you are Jona, a gust of air: a force of nature yes, but ultimately meaningless. But what you've started – the turning of the windmills – that truly frightens you. That makes you tense. You can see it for what it is. And for all your talk of change and agency, even you have the sense to be afraid for what lies on the other side of that."

Jona stared at him for a long moment, then turned and walked away.

Victor watched him go, then let his gaze shift to the half-eaten croissant. He eyed it suspiciously with one eyebrow cocked, then picked it up and finished it. As he was taking his last bites, the girl from the lecture came over to his table.

"Hi, my name's Tessa," she said, smiling from ear the ear with big cheeks that blushed a dusty rose color. "I haven't seen you around here before... I was wondering if I could sit down?"

Victor looked at her for a long moment, then got up to leave without a word.

CHAPTER 04

November 16th

Theo pushed his hair out of his face, glancing around with his jaw firmly set. He felt like he was playing dress-up, in his khaki coloured slacks and blue button down shirt, but in a way he had to admit he was. He didn't want to look like himself; he wanted to look put-together, as if he had his life figured out.

He pressed the remote lock button on his keychain twice, his rented silver two-door honking in response. His choices had been to either rent a car or hire a driver, and he didn't have the energy to bother with the small talk that would surely drift toward the reasons for his visit -- and Black Springs was anything but the ideal vacation destination. To visit Black Springs meant that you either had a dark spot in your past, or a very bleak future.

Theo felt the acute pinch of his new shoes as he climbed the steps to the complex. Nothing about the building seemed familiar to him, for which he was quite relieved. The sprawling building extended five stories, peeking above the tops of palms that sheltered glass balconies. Its modern modular design could almost be mistaken for some new money mansion, the clean lines and high fence surrounding the expansive property giving it an air of relaxation and privacy. He couldn't remember ever relaxing here though, just feeling incredibly numb or blindingly crazed.

Something about coming back of his own volition gave him power, however; and Theo found himself strengthen with every step he took. Pulling firmly on the large glass doors, he crossed the floor to reception in easy strides, masking any nerves with the charm of a boyish grin that had not found its way to his face for a very long time. When he reached the reception desk, he nodded at the tanned beauty absentmindedly sitting and tapping a highlighter against a stack of printed documents. She smiled in return, abruptly shaken out of a daydream by his arrival, and closed a document cover over the sheets to conceal whatever she had been working on.

"Can I help you, sir?" she asked, her smile widening as she straightened up.

Theo leaned against the desk, drawing closer to the woman. "Actually, you can. I'm here to speak with someone about my sister's health," he lied. "I'm supposed to meet with Nurse Feinberg, and I've just completely forgotten where my sister's doctor told me I could find her."

The receptionist smiled sympathetically. "Well, Nurse Feinberg has been a bit harder to track down lately. She's managing the whole ward up there now. It's close to lunch, so I'm sure she'll be in the group room on the fourth floor overseeing everything. When was your meeting with her for?"

"Two o'clock sharp."

The receptionist tittered, pressing a button on her headset and dialling an extension on her phone. "Yes, hi, can you remind Nurse Feinberg she has a referral meeting at 2:00?" she paused, glancing at her computer screen. "No, it's not showing on my schedule either, but you know how she's been lately… Yes, I'll issue the gentleman a visitor's pass now. One moment and I'll get you his name." She stopped talking and looked at Theo expectantly.

"Thomas Haven," Theo said, and the woman repeated the name into her headset. She smiled at Theo, a lock of hair escaping from her pinned-back bang and sliding across the bridge of her nose.

Pressing the button on her headset again, she exhaled deliberately. "Just let me get you your pass here now and you'll be all set to go up," she assured him, sliding her chair and typing at another monitor. The mechanical sound of metal chewing plastic emanated from a small machine hooked up to it, and a small card was spat out. She picked it up and gave it a once over before handing it to Theo.

"That'll get you into Feinberg's ward. It's locked to prevent any of the patients from wandering, so just make sure you don't lose that card, and don't hold the elevator or any doors for anyone who asks. Everyone's got to use their own key card, okay?"

Theo nodded, dropping the grin from his face. "I won't let you down," he said, tipping the card toward her as he backed away from the desk and turned toward the elevator.

"Fourth floor!" she said, standing up from her chair

and shouting the forgotten directions at him as he reached the button for the lift. He turned back to acknowledge her, nodding and smiling again before the doors opened allowing him inside.

Theo pressed the button labeled 4 and the elevator lurched to life. The doors shut smoothly, and in the confined space he could begin to catch the faintest whiff of rubbing alcohol. He shuddered at the smell, running his hand through his coifed hair and ruining his attempts at styling it. Being sent back up to the fourth floor after years away felt as if someone was prying the skin off his head with their bare nails. He felt raw, and beyond his disguise and his barriers he could sense the strength of the broken minds populating the building. He felt caught in a tsunami of emotion.

The elevator chimed a pleasant note and the doors slid open in front of him, allowing him to step into a small room with a door and card scanner. Until the elevator door closed, the light under the scanner glowed red, but once the doors slid shut the glow changed to a soft amber. Straightening his shirtsleeves and smoothing out his pants, he advanced on the card scanner. He almost expected for the receptionist to be in on some elaborate hoax to trap him back there. The thought alone made him feel paranoid and guilty. He held the card up to the scanner, and a soft buzz of the door electrically unlocking accompanied the change of the scanner's light to green.

Theo took a deep breath, composed himself, and pushed the door open and stepped back onto the fourth floor of the Black Springs Hospital.

CHAPTER 05

Floor Four

November 16th

Much to his surprise, the white ward looked almost inviting, with warm light spilling in from the large windows. In his memory, it was stark at its best and at worst it had been frigid. He surveyed the room intently, surprised to see and feel how calm most of the patients were. Even the jumbled, oppressive weight of their thoughts that he had felt so strongly in the elevator seemed light. Yes, many of them still broadcasted confusion and pain, but those feelings seemed to be mediated by comfort. Theo could feel his heart rate slow and his breathing calm, and only then did he realize exactly how tense he had been. For a moment, he wondered if returning here had been a mistake.

Theo shook himself off, making his way to the nurses' station. Three women busily pored over charts, chatting in hushed tones.

"And how is she reacting to her dosage, Nurse Clotho?" the oldest nurse asked, brow furrowed.

"Very well, I would say. I'll leave it to you and Nurse Lachesis though to speak to Nurse Feinberg if you dis-agree," answered the youngest nurse, her brown curled hair spilling down her back in such an elegant way she hardly looked as if she were wearing scrubs.

"No, I think we should give her a little more time on this dosage. She seems to be doing well. Nurse Atropos and I examined her earlier and she seems to be much im-proved," the third woman said, smoothing out her pris-tine white scrubs and turning to Theo. "Can we help you, dear?"

Theo smiled humbly at them. "Yes actually, I'm here for an appointment with Nurse Feinberg regarding my sister. The receptionist told me to come up here, but be-yond that I'm a little fuzzy."

"Oh, you must be the gentleman Patricia called up about. I can show you where Nurse Feinberg's office is," Nurse Clotho said smiling, breaking away from the other two nurses. "If you follow me, we'll be there in a jiff."

Theo obliged, following her as she ducked out from behind the nurses' station and headed down a hall on the left side of the room. Her brown curls bobbed behind her, almost beckoning Theo forward like some bouncing mes-senger.

They came to the end of the hall quickly, spilling out into a corridor twice as large. Nurse Clotho turned back to smile at Theo and make sure that he was still following her. "So, Thomas Haven, is it?" she said.

"Yes," Theo replied. "But Tom is fine really."

She smiled. "Well, Tom, it must be a while since you've been here. Nurse Feinberg couldn't remember who you were at first, then lit right up when she remembered."

Theo felt a lump in his throat.

"She'll just be a few minutes getting to you though; she said she had to go pull a few files from storage."

"Yes, well, my sister's health has been pretty good for a while, but lately she's taken a turn again. I wanted to come talk to Nurse Feinberg about possibly getting her in to adjust her medication."

Nurse Clotho's smile spread, and she came to a halt, putting her hand on Theo's arm. "I'm sure when your sister is well she appreciates you helping her. With Nurse Feinberg's help, I'm sure she'll feel better very soon."

Theo shifted uncomfortably in his shoes, and Nurse Clotho dropped her hand from his arm and let her intense gaze turn to the door in front of them, which she pushed open. She motioned for him to enter, smiling again as she closed the door behind him. "She'll just be a few minutes."

Theo found himself standing alone in Roberta Feinberg's office, not quite sure what to do with himself. The two wooden chairs that faced her desk looked stiff to sit in, and he could hardly deal with more discomfort at the moment. The collar of his shirt felt tight on his neck, the claustrophobic feeling that Black Springs gave him becoming recognizable once again. He forced himself to slow his breathing to rhythmic, deliberate draws that filled his diaphragm. He blocked out the buzz of psychic chatter that seemed to swirl around him, and placed a hand on the back of the chair to steady himself. He had become dizzy without realizing.

A water cooler stood next to the door, and he quickly

helped himself to a paper cone full of the cool liquid, then another, and another after that. He felt his cheeks cool, and he resolved himself to sitting in one of the chairs while he waited for Nurse Feinberg.

No sooner than he sat down did the door spring open, a stocky woman in dark blue scrubs and a mustard yellow cardigan waddling in. Her greying hair was pulled back in a tight bun, so tight that it seemed to pull her face taut. In the crook of her arm she balanced several thick yellowing folders, and in the other arm she juggled a coffee mug and a Styrofoam container. "Theo!" she beamed cheerfully, bumping the door closed with her bum.

"Good to see you, Roberta. Wish I could be visiting under better circumstances," he said, easing himself out of his chair and moving to help her with her load. He settled her coffee and the files on the desk as she made her way around to sit behind it with her lunch.

"I have to say, I'm happy to see you either way. You're looking so much better," she said, smiling and cracking open the lid on her container. Steam poured out, and little drops of water clung to the container where it had begun to cool. A thick roast beef sandwich and fluffy scrambled eggs lay inside, looking slightly shaken up from their journey to Roberta Feinberg's office.

"I'm feeling much better too," Theo smiled. "I'm glad you agreed to see me. Although, I do have a very big favour to ask."

Nurse Feinberg glanced up at him from over the top of the Styrofoam container, one eyebrow raised. "I'm listening," she murmured.

"I'm sure by now you've heard about the Port Haven

drama?" Theo asked.

She nodded stiffly, hesitating before loading eggs onto her fork.

"I'm sure you'll understand that because of that I have less people to turn to now for the sort of help than I used to," he paused. "And, honestly, right now I could really use some help."

"I'm listening," Nurse Feinberg mumbled, through a mouth full of egg.

"I need medical treatments for a friend of mine, but we need to leave town by the end of the week. Her condition is pretty volatile and we've exhausted our options."

"Is this connected to your big break from Port Haven? I'm not interested in diving head first into that sort of trouble," Nurse Feinberg said, sternly emphasising her words by jabbing her fork in the air.

"Completely separate, I promise. I'm getting as far away from the Port Haven mess as I can," Theo said, raising his hands defensively.

"Well then, that's reassuring. What's your friend's condition like? I assume it's not the standard stuff if you've decided to come back here."

"It's really not," Theo said, bowing his head and running a hand through his hair. "She's much more than I've ever really seen. It's hard to describe."

"Oh?" Nurse Feinberg's eyebrow shot up as her interest peeked.

"From what I can tell, it's some sort of molecular transformation. Her entire body just… it's like she melts into this black ooze."

Feinberg blinked.

"It's getting harder and harder for her to control though. She can't breathe when it happens and now it's taking all her energy to stay solid."

Feinberg stared at him for a moment, then remembered herself and swallowed. "Well... I can't guarantee results if she doesn't want to come down here and have testing done... but I may have a few injectables we could try with her." She put down her fork and started checking her drawers. "There's a new doctor here on staff who's been running a few experimental treatment programs in tandem with the school. I can try her on one of those, and if she wants to come in for a more specialized treatment we can give her a proper workup and customize something for her."

Theo hesitated. "We don't have much time, and I'm not sure she's going to want poking and prodding by strangers. This doctor is good though, is he?"

"Very," she smiled reassuringly, picking up her fork again. "Very trustworthy too. He's taken to the community very well."

Theo pursed his lips.

There was a part of him he had not used since stepping back inside Black Springs, the part of him that had made him special to the people at the Port Haven Institute, to Victor's needs, and even to some of the people at Black Springs. If he tried, he could open his senses, almost like a gate inside him, and see into other people's thoughts. They came displayed for him like billboards behind the people, those large digital billboards that changed their ad with the person's thoughts, and had audio and high def.

He had not used this part of himself since clicking the lock on his rented two-door in the parking lot. Opening the gate here was like holding the elevator door open, like the receptionist had warned him about: it let all the crazies in. Their thoughts rushed in like a wave, full of contradictions and logical fallacies and jigsaw pieces with no puzzle attached. Letting that much crazy in made you crazy.

But this was for Leigh.

Theo opened the gate of his senses just a little, prodding to check her honesty on the matter. He was still feeling fuzzy, but he pushed his conscious toward hers, opening himself up to her. Her mind comforted him on the worst days, with her tendency for clarity and openness. Today was no different, and he detected no hint of deceit or apprehension in her.

In his mind's eye, the wall behind her blinked away and turned on to a different channel, showing a reflection of his face back at him. She was in the moment, thinking of him. It was like looking in a mirror, if not a mirror distorted by her subjective opinion. He was prettier in the mirror than he really was, he thought, and younger. She saw him as he had been when she'd known him best, before the Port Haven School.

He relaxed instantly and recognizably, causing Nurse Feinberg to smile.

"You know, Theo, there's no reason for me to lie to you, but if that's what makes you happy I don't mind at all."

"Just a precaution," Theo assured her.

She nodded, laying her fork in her takeaway container

and reaching for the phone on her desk. "What I'll do for you is give Doctor Augustus a call now, let her know the situation; and she'll phone the prescription and instructions down to the nurses' station on this floor so you can just pick up the injections on your way out. If it works well, we'll set you up with a larger supply, but otherwise we may be able to arrange for a visit somewhere better suited to the two of you."

"Sounds good," Theo replied, getting up to leave again. He extended his hand and shook Nurse Feinberg's as she dialled the phone with the receiver nestled against her ear. She smiled at him again reassuringly, and he turned to leave.

"Take care, Theo. We'll do our best for your friend, I promise."

Theo exited Roberta Feinberg's office with a backward glance, catching her digging into her food as she mumbled instructions into the receiver. Shutting the door as he left, he was swept up in unexpected nostalgia. His time at Black Springs had been nightmarish at best, but he had been lucky enough to have Nurse Feinberg looking out for him.

At the time, she had just been a junior nurse, rough around the edges, but with a good instinct for treating patients that weren't responding well to the typical methods. Theo himself had been trapped in his own mind; although he barely realized it was a result of his emerging psychic abilities assaulting him. First he was overwhelmed with the thoughts of every person close to him, then, once he was committed, with the thoughts of every genuinely ill person inside Black Springs. Later, Nurse Feinberg told him how she had felt something was different about him, and after turning to the Internet for answers, had been contacted by Port Haven. Slowly she had opened the way for them to offer him alternative treatments and counselling, and he had been able to be discharged.

Little about that time brought back fond memories for him; for the most part he blocked his time at Black Springs out of his mind. Even still, memories of Nurse Feinberg coaxing him back into his own mind with paintbrush and acrylic trickled back to him. The smell of fresh paint seemed to fill his nostrils, and for a moment he felt a pang in his chest as he longed for the serenity those sessions had granted him. It had been so long now since he had needed to wash the crackling pigment from under his nails; such a long time since he had run his fingers over a fresh canvas, he longed to focus himself into his art. For now though, it would have to wait.

Theo's feet seemed to autopilot him back to the nursing station without difficulty. He barely remembered how he had got there when he entered the large room, now slightly more populated by patients enjoying free time. He made his way to the desk quickly, the brief daydream enough for him to let down his guard and find a stream of headache inducing thoughts pour into his own mind. Only Nurse Clotho was unoccupied by a patient, sitting behind the station with the glow of the computer screen illuminating her face.

"That was quick, Tom," she said, her eyes not flickering from the screen for a moment. "It will just take me a moment to get this prescription together." She rose from her chair and gave Theo a small, secretive smile, then turned to the wall of cabinets behind her and withdrew a ring of keys from a pocket in her scrubs. Theo watched, interest piqued, but was distracted by a hoarse fit of coughing close behind him.

He spun around, suddenly nervous that someone had gotten so close to him without him realizing, but relaxed when his eyes fell on the diminutive feminine form trying desperately to catch her breath. Her long dark hair bounced with each cough, and her olive skin looked pale, showing bruising easily. She shook with such force she seemed ready to fall over, and Theo instinctively reached out to steady her.

As he did so, she swayed, falling into his arms as if due to a magnetic pull. He was amazed at how light she was; her body should have been deadweight in his arms, but her burden was negligible. He slid to the ground with her, laying her out flat and tilting her chin back to open her airways. The shock of her sudden collapse and of the presence of thick purpled bruises roping around her neck, made his stomach roll and his guard drop.

Suddenly he saw water rushing at him. As if he was diving, he raced headfirst into dark, choppy water. He could feel water fill his lungs as if they were about to burst, cells fighting death and the sudden change in pressure. The pain was unbearable.

Abruptly, the scene was replaced with wailing car horns. His mind uncommanding, he felt his legs moving with purpose along a busy road. Vivid anxiety filled his chest as he spun his head not once, but twice, to verify a steady stream of traffic pouring toward him. He felt a sob catch in his throat as his body leaped unbidden into the deluge of cars, his ears suddenly overwhelmed by sharp honking, skidding tires, and the sickening crunch of bone.

Air escaped his mouth in wracking sobs, and the slick salt of tears rolled down his cheeks and blurred his vision. His hand moved to wipe his eyes, shuddering with each sob, but careful not to drop the pairing knife it grasped tightly. Vision clearer, he watched as the blade hopped along his skin, unsteadied by the force of his tears, before it finally found its mark and he was able to drag it smoothly across his flesh. The sting was minimal, and as blood began to well and pump out of his arm, he felt a quiet satisfaction. The satisfaction blossomed alongside self-loathing, and he added another slit below the first, then another, and another. The pattern of droplets settling on the cream mat below reminded him intensely of lace, but he barely had any time to analyze that realization before his vision blurred. He felt his knees give way as he crumpled.

Against cool white walls, he felt powerless. The walls towered over him as he sat on the floor, shredding the sheets around him into strips. He wound an end around each of his fists, pulling the fabric taut before bringing it around his own throat. His heartbeat screamed in his ears, pumping harder and faster, then slowing while his lungs screamed for air. As blackness closed around him, he saw Nurse Feinberg racing toward him.

Theo snapped from his reverie suddenly, still cradling the girl gingerly in his arms. Nurse Clotho swooped down in front of him, her brunette curls cascading around her head as she leaned over the girl, bringing a stethoscope to the crook of the girl's arm and taking her pulse. The lacework of freshly healing scars this act revealed sent another wave of nausea crashing over Theo.

"Will she be alright?" Theo whispered, as Nurse Clotho took the stethoscope out of her ears.

"Yes, it just looks like all the coughing caused her to pass out. She's recovering from a scare a few days back, but was showing steady improvement. Someone's on their way now with oxygen though, so we'll have her fixed up in no time," Nurse Clotho replied, her tone so calm and even that it was almost disquieting.

Theo gently raised the girl to a semi-seated position, resting her against his chest and cradling her carefully as he did so. The girl's eyes fluttered faintly, a soft green catching him off guard. She looked so young to be at Black Springs, though he shuddered as he realized he had probably looked that way when he was first sent there. In his peripheral, Nurse Atropos had appeared with the oxygen and, moving quickly in front of Theo, she slipped a mask over the girl's nose and mouth. "Mr. Haven, I'll ask that you hold that there for me a moment," she said sternly, her request more of an order.

For a moment, Theo forgot his assumed persona and stared blankly at her; however, Nurse Clotho shot him a pointed smirk, brow raised ever so slightly. He shook himself awake and cleared his throat, gently holding the mask in place and lowering his gaze again to the girl.

Apart from the bruising on her neck and scarring on her arm, other little details began to burst out at him as she woke in his arms. Dark circles under her eyes were almost masked by thick, long, lashes. The plain white t-shirt she wore looked too big for her by yards, and the soft cotton lounge pants she wore lacked any drawstring, clinging to her hips by force of elastic alone. Her nails were clipped down almost to the quick in a way that looked almost painful, but no doubt prevented her from doing any damage scratching herself.

On her wrist, a small band identified her as Alice V. Loveless and gave her date of birth. A quick calculation and Theo realized she was barely nineteen, though she could have easily passed for younger. He felt his heart go out to her.

She shuddered in his arms, coughing into the mask before breathing deeply. She drank from the machine hungrily, gulping in the oxygen and finding the strength to sit up. She glanced at Theo in confusion, but as she did so, Nurse Clotho and Nurse Atropos guided her to a waiting wheelchair, pulling her away from him. Seating her comfortably, Nurse Atropos wheeled the girl off while Nurse Clotho took Theo by the arm.

"My sincere thanks, Tom. Your sister must have truly excellent care with you around. Let me finish getting her prescription so you can be on your way," Nurse Clotho said as she led him closer to the medicine closet. She slid a rectangular box into a large prescription bag and handed it to Theo quickly, placing her hand on his back and guiding him back toward the door. "You'll find all the instructions you need in the bag, along with when to call us and what to look for. Best of luck," she said, ushering him through the doors and back to the elevator. The door had closed behind him before he even began to register everything that had just happened.

CHAPTER 06

Black Springs, Fifth Floor

November 16th

Caleb sat in his wheelchair, overlooking the Los Angeles skyline. There was a thick dark cloud off in the distance, hovering ominously just past Beverly Hills and virtually impenetrable to the naked eye. It loomed there like some spook or spectre, unwilling to venture any closer to the Black Springs Clinic, but making sure it was always visible at the same time… as if to say, "I'm watching you."

There was a bag full of liquid the color and consistency of piss hanging next to his chair, feeding down through a long tube and into a hole they'd plugged in his arm. He wasn't sure what it was for; it didn't seem to help any. The sclera of his eyes had gone a darkish gray and was often hard to see, his failing liver making what remained of the white a pale yellow instead. The skin around his eyes and mouth were so dry they cracked like desert ground, except for where there were sores. The sores were always moist, as though they sucked all the dampness out of the surrounding area and spewed it out in mounds of volcanic puss.

His hair was almost all gone. What remained clung around his ears, refusing to give up the ghost. He kept it slicked back, as though it were still a part of a larger whole.

His breath came in heavy, rasping wheezes that sounded like a car engine about to shut down for the last time. A plastic tube fed oxygen into his nostrils from a tank strapped to the back of his chair. It made a droning, predictable hiss every few seconds that was somehow impossible to tune out.

"Do you see that?" said an elderly man beside him, pointing to the dark cloud off in the distance. His name was Hector Kenworthy, and at one point in his youth he'd been a boxer. It was a point he often waxed on about at no end, either because he was proud of it or because he'd taken so many blows to the head that he didn't recall having mentioned it before. Caleb wasn't sure which.

He craned his head to see what the old man was gesturing toward, but did not speak.

"The Hollywood sign, you can't even see it. What's the god damn point of living in L.A. if you can't even see the damn Hollywood sign?"

He was right; the smog that wafted up from the ghetto blocked the Hollywood sign nearly in its entirety. Only a small section of the D was visible from where Caleb sat, and even that may have been a sliver of light reflected off one of the tall skyscrapers into his eyes. The sun was bright here – it was always bright here – and that made it no easier to see. His breathing got heavier for a moment, almost as if the effort of trying to focus his eyes exhausted him, and he sunk even deeper into his chair.

"I saw it for the first time in the 70s," Hector continued, leaning back and smiling wickedly as only an old
man caught in a scandalous memory could. "I was in town
for a match. Met a girl named Sandi and called her Sandra
Dee; whoo-boy, that girl was something else. Like she'd
been poured into her dress. Never once threw a fight, but
I would have to get a night with her. I used to be quite the
boxer."

Caleb said nothing and pressed a small red button on
his chair. A moment later, a nurse came out of the French
doors that led back into floor three. She took a moment
to look at the view, then turned and stood next to Caleb
with one hand on her hip. She was tall and leggy, made
more so by his perpetual seatedness. Her hair was brown
and short and always looked the same – whether that was
on purpose or if it just fell that way, he didn't know. He'd
seen her wear lipstick once and kept that memory, but
most days her skin was pale as though incapable of catching the west coast rays and her lips blended in so perfectly
they might not have existed.

"Had enough sunbathing for today?" Susan smiled,
even as she took the handles of his chair and started to
wheel him back into floor three.

As soon as he was inside he was blind, the brightness
of the outside no match for even the harsh fluorescents of
the inside. For a long moment he could see nothing, and
his eyes stung. He closed them and brought his hands up
to guard them. By the time his eyes stopped stinging, they
were past the porch and were in the hallway that led back
down to his room. "I've had enough of Hector Kenwor-

thy," he replied finally.

"Hector's a nice man."

"Hector never shuts up. You know that look you give someone when you want them to be quiet? He has no barometer for that. It's like he never learned what it meant."

She smiled. "You could learn a thing or two from him."

He looked over his shoulder at her as though he were going to respond, then turned back around and slumped his shoulders. When he sat like that the IV had a hard time getting the yellow piss that Doctor Augustus assured him was good for him into his veins, but he didn't care. The spot where the needle entered was beginning to sting already, and he ignored it. "How's Jillian?" he asked, resting one thumb against the other in his lap.

"She's good, she's happy. Still having some trouble reading though."

"Did you try Eric Carlyle?"

"She loved Eric Carlyle, thank you. I think she's finally starting to read the words, not just try to figure out what they are from the pictures."

"Hmn."

"She gets very frustrated though. The other day she was trying to read Brown Bear Brown Bear and she got so frustrated on the word purple that she started to cry and went into her room."

"Poor girl."

"Oh, that's not the worst of it. I followed her in a few minutes later. Turns out she's really worried her teacher's going to leave her behind. She's been getting up in the middle of the night and coming out to my bookcase to try and read the books, and she thinks she's stupid because she can't."

"Tisk."

"I still don't think she gets that those books aren't supposed to be read by little girls." She rolled him into his room, room 305, and parked him parallel to his bed. His head bobbed back a little when she stopped, like his neck did not have the ability to keep it straight. "Do you want to try to make it onto the bed yourself today?"

He stared past her to a painting on the wall. It was a large print of a Van Gogh wheat field. His vision was still tunneled and he couldn't see the frame, just her pale face and the wheat field behind it. She smiled at him, and the memory of when she'd worn the lipstick came to him. He was sure he could see her hair and the wheat move in the slight breeze that came west into the field. "I think I'll stay in my chair for a while," he said. He picked up the remote control from the foot of his bed and laid it in his lap without using it.

"There's a Duck Dynasty marathon on tonight," she smirked.

He shot her a wry look.

She laughed, then saw the tray from his breakfast out of the corner of her eye and took to picking it up. It had not been touched, and the stench of stale hardboiled egg had filled the room for hours. "I'll get this out of your way."

"Don't put yourself to any trouble."

She smiled again, then left the room. He listened to her heels as she made her way down the hall back toward the cafeteria. When he could hear her no more, he let out a deep, filling sigh and let his shoulders fall into his chair. He looked up at the wheat field, then took his remote and placed it back on the foot of his bed.

CHAPTER 07

November 16th

Theo fumbled with his keys, juggling the bag of medication and his coat in the other hand as he attempted to pick out the correct key for each lock on the apartment door. He had been gone slightly longer than he had intended due to the incident with Alice, and as a result had become caught in the snarl of commuters leaving Los Angeles for the day to return to the suburbs. He hoped desperately that all was well on the other side of the door, that the stress of Leigh's condition wasn't pushing her over the edge again. As he tried each key and failed, the tension overwhelmed him, and he dropped the key ring.

He slammed his open hand against the door, pausing for a moment to collect himself before laying the bag of medication and his coat gently on the floor and collecting his keys. He chose each key carefully this time, and one by one each of the three locks opened, finally allowing him inside.

The door opened to darkness; drapes lowered and lights dimmed throughout the entire place. Theo's heart sank, dreading discovering how sick Leigh had become while he was away. Was it another crushing migraine, leaving her unable to breathe? He hoped not. He hoped it was just that she was worn out and needed a nap. He called out into the silent apartment, breaking the monotony of the air conditioning unit quietly spitting out cold air. "Leigh? Are you alright?"

No answer came.

He locked the door behind him and raced, medication in hand, to the bedroom. He sped down the hall with a lump in his throat and worry creeping up into his chest. The door was ajar, so she should have easily heard him call to her. His heart sank. As quickly as he reached the door, he felt apprehensive now; his hand rested on the knob while he stood paralyzed, unsure if he really wanted to see what might be behind the door.

Theo closed his eyes and took a deep breath, centring himself. He opened his eyes and pushed the door open gently, bracing himself against seeing the worst. Instead, what he saw surprised him.

Leigh was nowhere inside.

He stared, puzzled for a moment wondering where she might be, then dropped the bag of her medication and ran room to room through the apartment. "Leigh? Leigh, where are you?" he yelled.

Again, there was no answer.

Theo doubled back toward the kitchen, checking to make sure she had not fallen. Not seeing her, he tore through toward the lounge, hoping she had just taken a moment to rest on the couch. Nothing but an empty room greeted him. Running out of options, he headed for the bathroom, heart pounding violently in his chest.

Again, the room was empty.

He sank down onto the cool tiles, head in his hands. A soft pinging noise drifted out of his pocket, cutting through his stress and bringing him back to life. Equally eagerly and fearfully he pulled out his phone. The message on the screen was equally calming and confusing though.

Since the incident at Shane Towers, Leigh had been despondent and had thrown herself into researching facilities that held the potential to heal her. She hadn't left the house for fear someone might recognize her from Shane or from the news. But now?

You were late. I'll be back soon.

Leigh Blackheart had never been someone who liked to take risks. She never was sent to detention growing up, never broke a rule, never put one toe out of line. She had always been ambitious though. Her need to impress figures of authority had been almost pathological; she had done everything in her power to rise to the top of her class. She studied long hours, read above and beyond assigned material, and whatever extracurricular activities she was involved with, she threw herself into practice. Anyone else would have burnt out under the pressure, but she had a tenacity that was rare. She had left her small town on a business scholarship to her top choice school, and from there she had only continued her upward path until she found herself at Shane Enterprises.

It was only then that her definition of 'whatever it

takes' became broader, and breaking rules became second nature. It was just part of the job.

Away from Shane though, she felt somehow less than herself. For the first time in her life, she was consistently confronted with things she couldn't control. Her old tricks – her wit, her intelligence, and her cunning – barely kept her afloat. Adulthood, for Leigh, was becoming a constant series of concessions made on where she was willing to draw the line.

She smoothed her periwinkle blue dress down over her legs, pursing her lips as she flattened out a stubborn wrinkle. She had made an effort today to powder her face a little darker and make her features a little softer, just to avoid any uncomfortable encounters.

She walked forward with feigned confidence, quickly ducking across the street to where the car was waiting for her. She felt as though she was sweating bullets, but her skin was dry to the touch. That alone made her more nervous. In the back of her mind, she was plagued by all the different ways the situation could deteriorate, the worst of which would be having an uncontrollable episode outside of the apartment.

Still, this meeting was necessary.

As she neared the car, the driver got out and opened the back door for her. He was a tall, lean man with white blonde hair and fine lines creeping into his features. He reminded her of Death. Not death the verb, Death the noun: the embodiment classically shown in a long robe with a scythe, but more modernly shown as a gaunt white man, the way he must have looked to the first peoples of Los Angeles.

She got in the car, dipping her head to avoid banging it. As she slid into the seat, Leigh felt vulnerable. The shutting of the door and the sudden darkness that followed as she was cut off from the outside did little to ease her mind, but she pushed those feelings down, smiling at the man she shared the backseat of the car with.

"Ms. Blackheart, a pleasure you could meet with us today," the man said, extending his hand toward her in greeting. He was a middle-aged black man, bald except for graying hair that clung to him around the ears. His facial hair was carved into a sleek goatee, but other than that his cheeks were a stubble-free sheen. His suit and tie barely seemed to fit around his tree trunk-like neck, though his clothes were clearly well tailored.

Leigh reached to take his hand in hers, and was taken off guard when he grabbed her wrist instead, forcing her palm up. She pulled her arm out of his grip instinctively, loosening the form of her hand to better slip through his fingers.

The man chuckled, throwing his hands up as if he meant no harm. She held her wrist in her other hand, her brow furrowing as she surveyed her companion's face.

"I hope you'll understand that I just wanted to see if the rumours were true. It's a curious ability you have, after all," he chuckled.

Leigh's tension relaxed a little in response to his explanation, but she still felt the hairs on the back of her neck stand on end. It had been a gamble to come out, and there was no guarantee he could actually offer her help.

"Mr. Hale, I'm sure you understand I've had a lot of offers lately," she began diplomatically, "and very few people have been able to show me any promise that their methods can help cure me. So far, everyone has wanted something from me and hasn't been able to deliver their end of the bargain. I need to know you're different."

Hale tapped the glass divider separating them from his driver and the car began to move. He relaxed in his seat, practically lounging as he studied her face. She felt as if he were waiting for her to crack.

"Ms. Blackheart, before your condition got out of hand, you were working for Shane. I'm told you were very good at your work there, and from what I've heard, your condition, if properly treated, could help you excel in a similar position. I'm not coming to you with a one-time deal here; I'm talking about a job offer that would be mutually beneficial in the long run. You agree to work for me at Circe, you get treated by our experienced team, not a bunch of scientists who think they can take a stab at curing you through trial and error."

"Again, I've heard similar stories before. I don't have the luxury of time to keep trusting people to deliver their end of the bargain eventually." Leigh looked almost like a cornered feral cat, perched on the edge of her seat regarding him without trust.

"In the circles I run in, you're making quite the name for yourself. You might not be the most... loyal employee that I could hope for, but you're driven to take care of yourself. That only works to my advantage if I continue to deliver what I promise you." A smirk played out on Hale's face as he said this.

"What is it you want from me then?" Leigh asked, taking a deep breath.

Hale extracted a syringe and vial from his jacket pocket and handed it to her. "I want you to take this home, take this, and meet me in the same spot in two days. If you like the effects, we'll talk about the sort of work I'm interested in you doing. I don't think it will be a problem though," he said smiling.

Leigh took the syringe and the vial in her hand, staring down at them. The milky liquid inside the vial swirled almost ominously. "How do I know this won't harm me?"

"You don't, Ms. Blackheart; but it's like you said already, you're running out of time. What do you have to lose?"

CHAPTER 08

Black Springs, Fifth Floor

November 17th

The fifth floor group room at Black Springs was a small white room with one cabinet nestled quietly in one corner and a large window opposite it. The window looked out onto the courtyard where people could be seen laughing and running and taking slow meaningful strolls with lovers and people they hoped to be lovers in the Los Angeles heat. Caleb faced it and watched as three men tossed a Frisbee back and forth on the green, stopping every once and again to admire a passer-by of the opposite sex. Caleb did not follow their gaze, just stared out the window with a young face that looked old for wear.

There were six of them in the room and one nurse, who was called a therapist only when they were in group and was just a nurse everywhere else. She had black hair and a metal paper-pad with heart stickers on the back. She sat across from him. Hector was to his immediate right, and then a Haitian man named Ruben. Ruben was missing all his hair, even his eyebrows. He looked sad all the time, and there were bruises wherever his flesh met itself: the crooks of his arms, his legs, even the folds of his cheeks.

To his left was Nadiyah, a young woman who didn't look like she belonged. She wore more makeup than even the most kept nurse. Her hair was back in a pony tail and her fingers twitched against her knee a lot. Next to her was Lori, a woman in her forties who was broad across the shoulders and looked strong despite the backless gown she wore that made it almost impossible to look strong. She moved her foot in small concentric circles on the tile in front of her, making a figure eight on its side with the skid marks from it. Next to her was a girl named Alice, who was strapped to her chair and seated closest to the Nurse. The straps were subtle, as though nobody else were meant to notice, but her fidgets and movements drew attention to them: fluid motions that were cut short by binding leather. She looked far too young to be there, but her presence meant that she should have been at least eighteen. There was a different group for people under eighteen.

The nurse, Bethany, looked across the circle at Caleb, holding the gaze. Caleb looked away at a random spot on the wall, holding one arm with the opposite hand.

"I kind of think I finally came to terms with it today," Lori said, staring at a fleck of white in the otherwise green tile between them. "My old partner came over to see me. He's this tall, handsome drink of water. Old as the hills. He came in with his daughter and her two kids to see me. They're sweet kids. Anyway, he was just yammering on about his day and started bitching about his new partner, some rookie from Queens, and it just sort of hit me: the world was moving on. I mean, when you get sick you expect your life to be there when you get better, but at some point the world just... moves on."

Caleb watched her and nodded when it was appropriate to nod, when everyone else nodded. His gaze shifted to Nadiyah. She was scratching at the crooks of her arm and there was dry, flaky skin coming off like dandruff that wasn't dandruff.

"I felt like that when they took the middle-weight belt from me," Hector said, taking the toothpick he was chewing out of his mouth. "They didn't ask me to defend that time, they just took it. I was a boxer. I fought in Vegas once, they still play it on highlight reels."

Nadiyah started to cry and got up immediately. She pulled her gown around herself and walked out of the room.

Alice turned to watch her go, moving slightly to gently stop her. The restraints stopped her from doing so, the movement barely noticeable.

The six remaining watched the empty space where she left the room for a moment, then one by one turned back to the circle. There was an invisible column between them that separated each, one from the other. The air between them was thick.

Caleb finally locked eyes with Nurse Bethany and focused on her. She fell into the background and all he could see was the green and the blue behind her, the sort of day when he wished the group room faced east. A red Frisbee danced up from the bottom right corner of the window, sailed along its path, and exited out the other side.

CHAPTER 09

November 17th

Victor pressed the answer button on his phone and a small blue logo appeared in the center of its frame, spinning in time with a series of rhythmic beeps and tones. It sat on its side, positioned in landscape mode, propped up at an angle by the small prong that came out of its back. He watched the logo buffer and spin, and reached out to adjust its angle, looking up at the fluorescent light above him with an annoyed glance.

Behind him he could hear water boiling, and the sound of tried herbs being rustled.

The beeping tones stopped, and after a moment there was a woman on his phone screen. She was fully framed, with just the hint of the table she sat at visible in the form of a wooden sliver across the bottom of the picture. She had dark hair that was cropped close to her head and clung to it steadfastly, and small, pursed lips. She looked at him through the screen emotionlessly for a moment, and then smiled. "Hello, Victor."

"Tasha," he smiled, leaning his hand against the crook

of his jaw. It was the most relaxed posture he had taken since leaving Arizona. A slight smile threatened to ruffle the edges of his facial hair, which was thick and straw-like.

She leaned in and squinted at the screen, looking to one side of it and then the next. "Have you arrived?"

"A few hours ago."

"How was your trip?"

"Hideous," he replied, without humour. "We encountered a man selling tacos whose entire family was living out of a U-Haul behind his cart. When he ran out of melted cheese on the one he was trying to sell to us, he scraped it off the one his son had been eating."

She laughed. "Lovely."

"Mnn," Victor hummed. "He was also harbouring repressed sexual urges that were making him impotent and I believe his wife was having an extramarital affair."

"Not that that matters."

"Not that that matters," he agreed, correcting himself.

He heard the sound of a spoon scraping china behind him and smiled, the smell filling his nostrils.

On the screen, a young blonde girl wearing a tank top and several belts appeared behind Tash holding a cup of tea. She came around to the front of the camera and placed it in front of her, her hair swinging back and forth like the golden pendulum of a clock as she did. Tash nodded in thanks and the girl stepped away, but stopped as she walked back out of frame to turn and smile at the camera.

"Kelly," Victor said and smiled in place of a wave.

Tash looked at the bottom of her screen quizzically and then raised an eyebrow.

As if summoned by her force of will, Jaycee appeared behind Victor and placed the tea in front of him with one shaking hand. When he was sure it was secure, he did not look to Victor for validation, but to Tash on the screen. "Chai karak tea, cinnamon stick shavings and black peppercorn infused with two milk and one sugar, water heated to ninety-eight degrees Celsius and milk heated to fifty degrees Celsius before mixing the two," he recited, counting each point on his fingers as he did.

"Thank you, Jaycee," Tash nodded, allowing the young man to step away.

Victor watched him retreat out of the corner of his eye, then smiled back at Tash. "That was cruel," he said with humour. "He had to make that in the bathroom of a Best Western."

She snorted, putting down her cup quickly before it sent her own karak tea jutting up her nose. "Civility is measured by what we do when it is not convenient," she said when she regained her compose. The words were undercut by her stifled laughter.

"You have whipped cream on your face."

"Enough," she laughed. "Enough."

He sipped his still-hot drink as he waited for her to compose herself. Once she had successfully taken a sip from her cup again, he asked: "How are the children?"

She swallowed, then nodded. "They're good. Kelly is good --"

"I saw."

"Mm well, she's doing quite well. Nick has been doing

well too; he has a renewed focus."

Victor raised an eyebrow.

"Not what I meant. Off topic, did you know he and Jaycee and Chad had joined some sort of online gaming... thing?"

"I hadn't taken notice."

"It's been making me go back and read Wayne Fife's work on imaginary worlds. Compelling things, really. The potential for studying epistemic cultural shifts in a controlled environment are limitless."

"Mm," Victor hummed in a non-committal way, taking another sip of his drink.

She eyed him for a long moment, a smile slowly appearing out of one corner of her lips. "I'm sorry, I know that makes you uncomfortable."

"Mn," Victor hummed again, putting down his tea. "It's fine."

She smiled restrictively. "How are Abby and Chad?"

"Good. They're in Salt Lake, visiting Koy."

"Family's important."

He nodded, staring at a place just behind his phone.

She watched him like that for a long moment, the intermittent blink of her short lashes the only indication that the video call hadn't frozen. Finally, she took a long gulp of her tea and picked up the paper in front of her that had heretofore been unseen. "Have you seen the reports for Maine?"

Victor snapped back to the screen, and took another drink from his cup.

CHAPTER 10

November 17th

Theo's eyes flicked open as he heard the click of the front door unlocking. He sat up quickly, brushing his hair out of his face as he did so. The once smart looking clothes he had worn to Black Springs were now crumpled and deeply wrinkled from his nap on the couch, and upon noticing this he hastily jumped up and struggled to straighten himself out. It did little good, and his furious attempts only increased the tension spreading through his skull.

Leigh walked into the dark living room fiddling with a small handbag, not paying the slightest attention to where she was heading. She moved gracefully through the dark, flowing blindly like water. There was something beautiful and magical about her, but it was the same sort of magic that seemed to keep her foreign to Theo. In the weeks that they had spent together Theo had been an open book for her, but she hadn't exactly returned the favour. He had no doubt she was more open with him than perhaps anyone else she had ever met, but the undercurrent of secrecy troubled him more and more each day.

Theo cleared his throat as she almost walked past him, head still turned down into her purse. The noise caused her head to flick up quickly, and in the dark, her deep doe eyes met his.

"God, Theo, you frightened me half to death. What are you doing out here in the dark?"

"I've been waiting for you. Where the hell have you been?" he shot back angrily.

"I'm sorry, I texted, I-I didn't think it would be a big deal…" she stammered, only to be cut off.

"Of course it's a big deal, Leigh. Your face is plastered in the news right now! What if someone were to see you and call in a tip?" Theo shouted.

"Keep shouting; maybe you'll tip them off yourself" Leigh hissed, seeming to loom toward him ominously.

Theo held his temples with his hands and closed his eyes. "I'm sorry, I've just been freaking out here. It's been a rough day."

Leigh leaned back, softening only slightly. Her mouth was still set in a firm, straight line, and her eyes had a steely quality to them that dissuaded Theo from making another outburst. "What did you do today then? You were gone on errands so long, and I couldn't wait around all day for you to come back."

Theo let out a long sigh, collapsing onto the sofa and burying his head in his hands. "I met with some old contacts from my time at Black Springs. Went back there, actually. It didn't really seem real."

"Why the hell were you back there? That place still gives you nightmares, for Christ's sake." Leigh's brows furrowed as she stared intently at Theo, and she moved to sit on the couch across from him.

"I couldn't leave town without trying to find another option for you. It feels like we've tried everything at this point. It's almost every night now I wake up to you choking. What else was I supposed to do?" Theo raised his palms apologetically.

"You're not my keeper, Theo!" Leigh snapped. "You could just let me handle it!"

Theo's features seemed to sink in his face, and his shoulders slumped, making Leigh regret the outburst. There was nothing in the world that should have automatically made them allies, not even their abilities. From where she stood, he was loyal to her without any reason for it. She couldn't help but feel that that loyalty was misplaced.

"Maybe you're right, Leigh. Maybe I shouldn't bother. But last time you tried to handle this, innocent people got hurt. We can't keep making those kinds of mistakes."

Theo's words cut her like a knife. "There wasn't any 'we' in that, Theo. If you hadn't tried to come save me, you wouldn't have been involved at all," Leigh paused, her words digging in deep and bruising his heart. He had thought they were a team. He had thought she cared. He'd even gone to Black Springs for her, the place of his nightmares, the place where-

And with all that hurt boiling inside, his anger bubbled over: "Believe what you want then! I go out of my damn way to try and save you because I thought 'we' were in this together!" He got up; grabbing the bag of medication he had gotten from Black Springs, he flung it on the coffee table separating Leigh from him. "Here's your damn medicine. I've had more than enough bullshit for one day."

"What do you mean?" Leigh asked, the bite disappearing from her voice.

"I mean I'm fucking sick of your attitude, when I'm putting myself through hell and you're just stringing me along!"

"God, no, I'm sorry. I didn't mean that. I meant: what do you mean 'my medicine'?" Leigh hung her head, casting her large dark eyes upward sadly.

Theo sighed, willing away the anger, and sat down on the sofa once more. "I mean, I explained the situation to my contact, they spoke to a doctor that deals with Port Haven, and they sorted out their best guess for you. You have a couple days to take it; depending on how you feel, we can go get more or we can go in and have them run tests. We have just enough time to do this before we have to leave L.A.; I just need you to have a little faith in me."

She was suddenly acutely aware of the vial and syringe in her handbag. "Theo, I, I can't just take some random medication. The, the side effects could make things a million times worse, I, I… I could die," she stammered

"Leigh, you could die without them at this point. What do we have left to lose?" Theo pleaded, taking her hands in his own. She met his eyes reluctantly and stole herself against his more effective methods of prying. "I know you're scared, I know you don't want to let me in, but please try it."

It was Leigh's turn to sigh now. "What makes you think this will work?" she asked.

"You're not the only person with abilities Black Springs

has managed to help before. Nurse Feinberg was always so good to me, and she trusts this doctor. She says he's worked well with Port Haven, so he's not going to rat you out to Shane or anyone, and I'm pretty sure she's actually treating more people with abilities at the moment. There was this girl today... I don't know how anyone could survive everything she's survived and not have some incredible gift."

"Modern medicine is pretty remarkable; she may just be lucky. Don't wish a 'gift' on someone when it might turn out to be more of a curse," Leigh said darkly.

"Anything she's been through; she should have died. I wouldn't call survival a curse," Theo countered. "What's that old saying, getting old is a privilege denied to many?"

"Well, if you ask me, being able to die is a privilege in and of itself. With everything you've seen me go through, don't you think being able to die with some form of dignity is important?"

Theo sighed. "I guess. I just don't see myself ever being able to give up fighting. I would rather die fighting to live than give up."

His tone hadn't been judgmental, but the moment the words left his lips he could tell he had hurt her. Her eyes had clouded over, the light that usually made them look so glossy and doe-like disappearing. "I hope you don't think I want you fighting my battles for me, if that's the attitude you have," she said bitterly.

"Leigh, please, I didn't mean it like that," Theo apologized, moving to stop her as she began to get up and leave the room.

"Please don't. I can look after myself, Theo. I'm not some damsel in distress," she said, pulling away from him.

"I'm sorry, I really am. I never said you were. I just want to help," Theo pleaded. "Please, there's a real chance that these pills from Black Springs could help you get better. Your outlook doesn't have to be so bleak."

He held the bag of pills out to her in one hand and held the other palm out, inviting her back toward him. She glared daggers at him, snatching the bag from his hand, but didn't return to his side. "I'll decide my outlook on my own. Pills won't change that, even if they make me better," she snarled.

Theo watched, shell-shocked as she stalked out of the room. He barely registered hearing her slam the bathroom door, and by the time he had stumbled onto the balcony to try and catch a breath of fresh air, he was too far away to hear Leigh flush the pills down the toilet.

CHAPTER 11

Black Springs, Fifth Floor

November 17th

Susan wheeled Caleb back out onto the patio. The night air was cool and refreshing, kissing his skin. He could barely feel it. The moon was high and orange; a farmer's moon, his father would have called it, if his father had still been alive. He watched it for a long moment with Susan standing erect behind him.

"It's beautiful," he said, his voice a hushed whisper.

She placed a hand on his shoulder. "I'll leave you to enjoy it."

He turned to protest, but she was gone.

There were three other men on the patio. Hector sat in his wheelchair and puffed on a cigar, letting the smoke curl around his head like a wreath.

"Should you be smoking that?" Caleb asked.

Hector laughed, and it erupted into a cough. When it passed, he smiled at Caleb with a grin that seemed too big for his face. "What are they going to do? Kill me?"

Caleb grinned back and nodded.

The other two men weren't in wheelchairs; they sat on the bench that looked out over the city. The one furthest away was hunched into himself. He was bald and his eyes had long ago gone jaundice. His nose was a pair of truncated nostrils that stopped short of a mouth that looked like a slit in his face, without lips or indentation of any kind. His shirt hung loose on him, and despite the tautness of his arms, he looked malnourished.

The other man sat tall, at least a head and a half over the first. He sat with his arms stretched out over the back of the bench in possibly the most relaxed pose Caleb had seen since he'd come to Black Springs. He had long hair that came down past his shoulders and sharp cheekbones. He wore a black shirt that was almost too small for him, his muscles pressing against them. His chest was firm. He looked for all the world like a Viking in jeans. There was an ignored cell phone sticking out of his pants pocket with a blinking green light.

Caleb threw a quizzical glance at Hector, who shrugged happily. He turned back to the Viking. "Don't believe I've ever seen you around here. And no offense, but you don't look like you belong in palliative care." He nodded toward the other. "Him, maybe."

The man turned as minimally as possible. "We're just visiting." He stuck out his hand. "My name is Victor. "

He shook it. "Caleb Galen."

"Jean-Claude Maximus," the bald man spoke up, giving a friendly salute. "You can call me Jaycee."

Caleb grinned, then turned back toward the skyline.

Victor watched him for a long moment. There was intent in his eyes, a small glint and a smile tickling at the edges of his lips over and over again. He opened his mouth to speak, closed it, and then tried again: "It's a lovely view."

Caleb looked out over the view. "It ought to be."

Jaycee watched Victor as he inched closer and closer to the edge of the bench, until he thought he might fall off. They sat like that for some time, the cool breeze coming off the patio and pushing back the slight wisps of hair that clung around Caleb's ears.

Hector wheeled over to face Caleb, their chairs perpendicular to each other. His chair squeaked until he stopped, his toes caught between the spokes of Caleb's chair. "See those lights over there?" he said, cocking his head toward a dull throb of amber in the distance.

"Yeah?"

"I used to box there. Once I went me nine rounds with a fellow named Estevez. He knocked me clean at the end of the ninth, but it was a good match, I liked the match. That was when boxing was just boxing, none of this UFC stuff. I like UFC, but it's not boxing. That was boxing, just who could hit harder."

Caleb frowned, then turned his chair away without a word. He thumbed the red button on the arm of it, and when the door to the fifth floor did not open immediately, he sighed.

Victor tilted his head, his eyebrows pressing upward in the center of his brow. He rose to his feet.

"Boxing, huh?" Jaycee chimed in, leaning forward on his knees. "I like boxing. Were you any good?"

Hector smiled. "They used to call me Vector. You never knew where I was coming from. I can use both my hands;

I'm... I'm ambidextrous. That's the word."

Victor stepped over to Caleb. "Do you need a push back to your room or something?"

Caleb looked him up and down, glanced back at the glass pane door Susan was not stepping through, then nodded. "Sure."

Victor smiled and took him by the handles. Jaycee followed not long after, once Hector finished his sentence explaining why he should have won that fight against Romerez that one time in Atlantic City.

There was a television on in the foyer playing reruns on the Hallmark channel. Roma Downey looked out into the viewer and was surrounded by soft light. She was saying something, but the mute was on. Her mouth moved in strange shrinking circles when she said words with an Oh-sound in them. There was no one watching it, and the captions weren't on.

"You were getting agitated in there," Victor said under his breath as he pushed the chair into the hall.

It took Caleb a moment to realize he was speaking to him, and not to Jaycee. "Um... sorry?"

"Nothing to be sorry about."

"He does that a lot, the talking about the boxing. He never shuts up about it, actually."

"He's lonely, but he's happy. Talking makes him happy, and so does being listened to."

"If I were to have made it to that age, I'd have hoped I would have had more stories than that."

Jaycee snorted.

"Turn here," Caleb said. "It's 305."

"I'm sure he's got some stories," Victor said, his smile

fading. "If you collect enough good ones, you never want to tell them ever again."

Caleb's brow furrowed.

"I get it though. Sometimes I can't stand people. Sometimes. I was always like it though. Sometimes I blame it on the service, but really the service was a product of it, not the other way around."

Jaycee turned and tilted his head at Victor. He had never heard him speak so much about himself before.

"Were you always like that too?"

Caleb was quiet for a moment, his body shifting down. Victor watched him. After a long pause, he simply said, "No."

They continued in silence until they were in the room. Victor looked at the wheat field painting for a long moment and stroked his beard. Jaycee shifted uncomfortably from foot to foot.

There was another tray full of food resting at the bedside table. Victor eyed it, then eyed the urine-coloured liquid slowly being dripped into Caleb's veins. "Takes away your appetite, huh?"

He nodded.

"Maybe it's just the food," Jaycee laughed. "The nurses seem nice, but I've eaten in a cafeteria. You'd be better off down the road at Rotten Ronnie's."

"There's a great diner down the road, Lacey's, I think it's called. If you like, we could bring you back something from there tomorrow."

Caleb looked at them long a hard, but the moment Victor had mentioned "diner," he had begun to salivate. He looked away from them toward the window that looked out to where the Hollywood sign should have been and swallowed. He nodded.

Victor smiled happily and slapped Jaycee on the back. "It's a deal then. We'll be back tomorrow with a pierogi. You'll love them; they're full of grease, but they taste light."

He left the room before Caleb had an opportunity to reconsider.

CHAPTER 12

November 17th

The night air was cold on his skin, but Theo barely noticed it. Sometimes it felt like the last few years of his life had been some sort of bizarre dream. When he had begun hearing voices during university, he had tried to just brush it off, but his plummeting grades had put him on academic suspension, and his roommate's complaints to housing about his erratic behaviour had resulted in a temporary psych hold and a visit from his parents. He didn't doubt that his mother's fear upon seeing his state was rooted in the love she had for him, but it had been different with his father. His fear upon seeing Theo's condition was no doubt rooted in concern for his own public image, and there was no better way to deal with that than by locking his son away in the cushiest, most private medical facility he could find. It didn't phase him when Theo's condition had worsened inside Black Springs; and once Theo had finally gotten better, his first priority had been to throw as much money as it would take at his son to keep him away.

As Theo made his way down the fire escape, his father's contempt was all he could think about. Theo didn't have any delusions that at any point he had been some shining joy in his father's life, but rationalizing the utter rejection was still difficult for him. During his childhood -- during his father's rise through politics -- his father had made sure to publicly portray the image of a man with a close bond to his family. He had actually always been more interested in his work, but Theo had been able to look back on those public outings fondly. Having a son with a schizophrenia diagnosis had been a good ploy for public sympathy, but beyond that it was a convenient excuse to stop keeping up the pretence of a close father-son bond. Theo coming back into the picture at any point was basically just a complication at this point, one that his father didn't need. Or at least, that was the way Theo saw it. He couldn't know for certain anymore, he had barely seen the man since his powers had begun to manifest and was glad for the space between them.

The metal grating of the fire escape clanged with each of Theo's footfalls. He needed to be out of the apartment, somewhere where the tension hanging in the air wasn't quite so palpable. He wondered if maybe there wasn't something wrong with him that made it so easy for people to push him away. For all the time he and Abby had spent together in Port Haven, she had all but forgotten him when Hunter appeared on the scene. Now Leigh was pushing him away too, and it didn't seem to matter how many sacrifices he was willing to make for her. He was starting to feel like at the end of the day he would only ever be able to rely on himself.

Theo exhaled his frustrations slowly as he neared street level. His anxiety from visiting Black Springs, and then from finding Leigh gone, still seemed to be circling in his body. A pit of pressure twisted in his gut and he felt the familiar pull of his chest muscles tensing involuntarily. He hit the last level of the fire escape harder than he meant to, and sent the ladder crashing toward the street in a violent cacophony of metals scraping against each other.

He clambered down quickly, almost slipping as his foot hit the last rung. It made his heart dart up into his throat. He gripped the railing firmly, holding himself steady for a moment before lowering himself to the ground.

Feet on the pavement, Theo began walking. His suit billowed in the breeze, and his tie licked at the night air. His shoes pinched as he walked, but he pushed that annoyance to the back of his mind. They were running out of time, even without his father's deadline, and this kind of fighting wasn't about to help them accomplish anything.

Theo found himself headed for the Thai takeout several blocks over. As he neared the restaurant, the scent of sweet spices and cooking oil wafted out to greet him. In the time it took to reach the door, the scent overtook his nervous thoughts and calmed him. He breathed a sigh of relief when he entered the restaurant and found it empty, save for a young Filipino man mopping the front and the elderly chef out back. The boy smiled when he saw Theo, and moved to place the mop behind the counter. "Two number eights to go again tonight, Mr. Theo?" he asked, getting ready to punch in the order on the till.

"Just the one tonight, please Joe," Theo replied, handing the man a few bills out of his breast pocket to cover the meal before pulling up a chair and settling in to wait for his order. He stared out the window into the inky darkness that bathed the city, the yellow glow of streetlamps burning faint holes in the night. He sighed as he scanned the street, but nothing in particular caught his eye. Parked cars lined the sides, and the only person he could see was feeding his nicotine addiction on the stoop of an apartment building. Theo rubbed his eyes with the balls of his palms, slumping over the table in front of him.

The sizzling sound of meat and vegetables on the flat-top created a calming white noise for him, allowing him to relax as Joe mopped around him. The lemon scent of the cleaner in the mop water mixed pleasantly with the salty savoury aroma of whatever sauces would cover the ribbon noodles that were surely boiling away out back.

Theo caught a glimpse of his own reflection in the napkin dispenser in front of him. He looked about as terrible as he felt, but he supposed that was no surprise. Joe's respect for his privacy tonight, when they may have traded jokes about their respective days another night, was something he appreciated immensely. Theo simply did not have the energy to come up with a decent lie to explain what surely looked to Joe like a hellish breakup between two of his regular customers.

Theo lost himself in thought, staring at his own distorted and tired looking eyes in the napkin dispenser. All he wanted to do was wake up feeling rested and discover that the last few years had all been some sort of weird dream. He couldn't actually pinpoint a time in the past that he would like to go back to, a time where he considered himself happy, but he would have settled for uncomplicated, that was for sure. He let out another sigh.

"Mr. Theo?" Joe asked, causing Theo to jump in his seat. "Your order's ready to go."

"Thanks, Joe," Theo replied, forcing a smile for the concerned looking cashier. He pushed himself up out of the chair and took the brown paper bag from Joe's outstretched hands. He headed for the door, turning around and pushing it open with is back. "You have a good night, Joe. Get home safe," he said, nodding at the man as he left.

Theo stepped back out into the cool night air and surveyed the street, debating where to head next. The smoking man across the street still sat puffing slowly on a cigarette, though now he appeared to scrutinize Theo's unkempt midnight appearance.

Theo hurriedly decided to make his way toward the nearby park. He had no desire to head home at that moment, and the fresh air helped to wake him up. For a moment, he seriously considered finding the closest rental option for the night, but discarded the idea for all the hassle it would be.

He walked absorbed in thought for some time, until he became aware that the hairs on the back of his neck had begun to stand on end. As he neared the park, he became aware of how poorly lit it was, and glanced around nervously. He didn't see anything at first, but the flicking sound of a lighter made his head flick around once again.

His eyes finally settled on the flame about fifty feet behind him on the opposite side of the street. Leaned against a bus stop was the same man from the stoop. A halo of smoke drifted above his head, catching the streetlights and illuminating his face.

Theo doubled back, pushing into the man's mind. The man's satisfaction was front-and-centre as the cigarette smoke soothed the snarling pangs of hunger in his gut. Theo visualized moving that thought to the side, searching for the man's intentions.

"You're following me," he snarled, getting closer to the man and still prodding for information. He caught a flash of himself and Leigh through the window of the Thai takeout, from the man's perspective. A camera lens clicked. Another memory, one of an office and men and women in well-tailored clothes, crowded in, and Theo found himself looking down at the scene again, this time printed and lying on the desk in front of the man. "He sent you to spy on me, didn't he?" Theo spat.

The man began to stammer. "You've got it wrong, man; I'm just waiting here for the bus. Christ, calm down."

"You're lying," Theo hissed, getting uncomfortably close to the man. "If you think for a second you can fool me, you're the fool here."

"Like I said, man, I'm waiting for the bus. I don't know what you're talking about. Don't make me call the cops," the man sputtered, dropping his cigarette.

Theo glared at him. "You can tell my father I don't need to be tailed. I'll be gone like he wants. Stay out of my business."

The slow squealing of brakes broke Theo's concentration, and for a second he turned to look and see where the sound was coming from. A city bus pulled alongside them, and by the time Theo spun back around, the man was already through the door and up the steps. Theo cursed.

The bus pulled away as the man sat down, staring out the window at Theo with pursed brows and apprehension. He had to wonder in that moment if he was just losing it again, if maybe the paranoia and anxiety were getting to him and affecting his abilities. He rubbed his brow with his free hand.

He was tired, exhausted even. He needed to eat. He needed a proper night's sleep. He sighed, and headed back toward the park to settle down with his food.

On the bus, the man let the mask of fear drop from his face, and pulled out a phone. "I've had to break off surveillance, sir. The boyfriend caught on to me. He has no idea who I'm working for though. He thinks it's his father. We're still good." The man paused, listening to the voice on the other end of the line. "Yes, Director Hale, of course. I'll be in touch again shortly," he said, hanging up and letting his mouth fall into a grim line across his face.

CHAPTER 13

Black Springs, Fifth Floor

November 18th

Caleb opened his mouth wide to fit in the sandwich and still could barely do so, managing to only take a small corner out of it. It wasn't a pierogi; it was roast-beef on white and the beef was piled high and folded onto itself with mayonnaise dripping out the back in gargantuan globs every time he took a bite. There was an extra slice of bread in the middle that had been soaked in warm, meaty gravy. It squished against his teeth when they reached it, sliding through easily after the pull of the beef and the crunch of the shredded lettuce.

Victor sat on the edge of the bed eating his own. Though his sandwich was just as big, he held it easily with one hand, and it was only then that Caleb saw just how massive the man's hands were. They were like paws. The other one, Jaycee, stood against the wall in the corner. He was missing fingers on each of his hands, but there weren't stubs where fingers should have once been.

"How do you like it?" Victor asked, nodding toward

to sandwich.

Caleb moved to speak, then placed his hand in front of his mouth to stop crumbs from escaping. "It's good. It's very, very good."

Victor nodded happily and gave his leg a friendly, tapped punch. He let his eyes sway around the room when he realized he was watching the other man eat. All three of them took a bite; Jaycee was almost done already.

His eyes fell once again upon the Van Gogh Wheat Field, bolted at its four corners to the wall just to Jaycee's left. The blue of the sky seemed to have been scraped on, leaving uneven trails of paint that started thick and then thinned out to near transparency the further they went to the left. It seemed like wind, like the wind was blowing in great blusterous gusts that might have taken Jaycee into the air like a kite had his feet not been so firmly placed on the ground.

"Where are your parents at anyway?" Victor asked, not tearing his eyes away from the Van Gogh until the question was done. His Southern drawl had come through more than it usually did, and it made both the young men with him tilt their heads.

"My father died when I was young," Caleb replied without emotion on the matter.

"You're young now."

"No, when I was about three. My mother works out of state, she'll be in someday soon I'm sure. Maybe. It's long hours, she does what she can."

Victor nodded. "My father died when I was pretty young... not as young as you were, mind, but young all the same. Sometimes I'm not sure if I remember him right.

I'm not sure if my memories are my own or they're just things that got told to me... you ever get that?"

Caleb looked down at his sandwich, took another small bite, then laid it back down on the Styrofoam plate it had come in. "No, I didn't really know him. My mother says I'm like him though. She said anyone that knows me also knows my father. Anyone who sees me also sees my father."

"That's sweet," Jaycee said, a smirk tickling the edge of his lips. "My mom never said anything like that about me and my dad... or at all, really."

Victor nodded. "You're not from Los Angeles then?"

"Sacramento," he said, motioning to the black hair that clung to his ears as if it explained something of his origin. "We travelled a lot though. I can't say there's any place I'd call home." He stopped and smiled. "Except the tent. We had this tent, I think I spent most of my time in the tent."

Victor smiled and nodded once, then took another bite of his sandwich.

The door opened and Susan walked in, pushing a trolley that looked like the type flight attendants used when they went up and down the halls of a plane, the type that always managed to bash you in the shin no matter how tightly you tucked in your legs. She stopped short when she entered and looked at Victor and Jaycee, as if not sure she was in the right room until her eyes fell on Caleb. "Well, you're popular today," she smiled, starting to walk again as though she were on a track that had hit a momentary hitch.

"I wouldn't go that far," Caleb smiled. Victor watched

him, then turned back to the Nurse. She was tall, most of her height coming from her legs. She had brown hair she kept up with only small wisps escaping and playing with her cheeks. She had hazel eyes, and her lips were thin.

She eyed the sandwich that now sat sideways on Caleb's lap, and smiled. "You've got him eating?" she asked, turning to Victor.

Victor regarded her for a moment, then smiled. "What little he's eaten, yes."

"I'm going to finish it," Caleb assured. "First real food I've had in months. Maybe I should follow it up with some wine."

She laughed, then picked up a tray of food off the trolley and laid it on the bedside table. "I'll leave this here in case you want it later." She went back to the trolley and returned with a clear bag so full of the clear yellow fluid that it bulged.

The room went silent for a moment. She stood between the trolley and Caleb, holding the bag like a limp newborn against her chest.

Caleb looked at the bag hanging by his bedside, and saw that it was nearly empty. His face drained of color and emotion as she stepped up beside him and began to unhook the limp, deflated bag.

Jaycee watched for a moment and put his sandwich aside, shuffling his feet from one side to the other. "We can leave if you like."

Victor turned and shot him a look.

"It's okay," Caleb said. He winced as the old bag came loose, tugging on the cord that went to his arm with its last act and yanking the needle to one side. He hissed and bit his lip.

"Sorry, sorry," Susan said, a patch of gauze in her hand immediately and pressing against the spot to stop the bleeding. Her free hand went to his shoulder, so swiftly and gently neither even realized it was there. Victor watched this, her thumb resting on the thin, gaunt muscles of his chest. Her nails were painted white, except the thumb, which was white with a red cross on it.

"It's okay," he said again, his voice softer than it had been and somehow lacking the raspy quality it had since he'd been admitted.

She pressed hard on the gauze, then pulled it back, examining the area underneath. There were several small droplets of red on the underside of the fabric, and the needle was out, dribbling the last of the yellow bile from the first bag onto his arm. It smelled horrible, like garbage left out in the hot sun for too long.

"I'm so sorry," she said, even as she disposed of the needle in the bright yellow medical waste bin above his bed. She retrieved a new needle from a drawer and unwrapped it with one clean motion and brought it to his arm. She hesitated, bringing the needle's tip to his flesh three times and depressing it before finally biting her pale lips and sliding it in. Caleb flinched, unable to watch and looking sheepish about it. Victor watched it all.

She finished hooking up the new bag of fluid, and made sure it hung well before she stepped away from his bed.

"I think I've done enough damage for one day," she laughed nervously.

"Not at all," Caleb replied, laying his head back onto

the pillow. The event had exhausted him, and his breath was heavy. The Styrofoam plate holding the sandwich was now next to him on the bed, tilted to one side and laying in a pool of its own gravy. He eyed it suspiciously now, the new yellow bag dropping furiously for its fullness.

Susan eyed the sandwich as well. "Let me know if you start to get nauseous," she said softly. "The beef won't be easy if it comes back."

Jaycee looked down glumly. "I'm sorry; we should have thought-"

"It's okay," she smiled, politely but fake. It was the smile you gave to a stranger you bumped into on a train. She turned back to Caleb and the smile became genuine. It made her face glow from the cheeks out. "Let me know if you need anything. Is Big Brother on tonight?"

He nodded.

"Maybe I'll step in and catch a bit."

"I'll PVR it."

"Don't bother."

"It's no bother."

She smiled and left the room.

Victor looked down at the remainder of his sandwich. It no longer looked appetising, the putrid stench of the yellow medicine still hanging in the air and making everything smell bad. He pushed it away and turned back to Caleb. "She seems nice."

Caleb smiled. "She's very nice."

"She likes you."

He snorted and turned away, back to the rolling fields of wheat. Jaycee stepped between he and the painting, and for an instant it looked as though Van Gogh had painted him there, his exaggerated features and patchy skin fitting in so well with the fields and sky that they may as well have been created with Van Gogh's own hand.

"You like her," Victor continued, getting up from the bed and stretching his limbs. The phone in his pocket vibrated, and he ignored it.

Some color returned to Caleb's face.

"She's pretty cute," Jaycee smiled, stepping forward. "Seems nice too. Got one of those smiles you just can't fake. I've got a girl back home like that."

"Then I don't know why you're here," Caleb said, laying his head back on his pillow. It was tilted back and the color left his face again, suddenly looking very dry. His eyes were open but lost all response to Jaycee. "I used to have women, but I never had a woman. If that makes any sense."

Jaycee nodded. "Makes perfect sense."

His eyes shut half way, as though he were caught between reality and a memory. "The women used to come to the tent all the time, always in these wonderful Sunday dresses. The tent was so hot and everyone would just pile in there and everything was covered in sweat. There's something about a woman covered in sweat."

Jaycee nodded.

"What was the tent for?" Victor asked, his voice low and firm.

"We used to travel around with it, sleep in it and perform in it, put off shows. People would come for miles, some because they loved us, and some because they hated us; but once the lights came on and the mike got tapped, they were all quiet. Except when they sang. You ever hear that many people sing? Beautiful sound. And there was me, up at the top of it all. Everyone's eyes on me. For first impressions, confidence is everything to a woman. I was there in my element at the front of the crowd, all eyes on me. I must have looked like a rock star. And man oh man, did the women flow. Like water."

Victor smiled. "What did you perform?"

"Perform may not have been the right word," he coughed. His voice had become a harsh whisper. "I tried to help people. Didn't always work. But I tried, and people laughed and smiled and – it was good. It felt like I was doing good."

Jaycee raised an eyebrow. "You were a faith healer?"

Victor turned over his shoulder and shot him a look.

"I guess you could call it that. Yeah. Don't get the wrong idea though. Religious guy talking about getting laid - that wasn't me."

Victor narrowed his eyes.

"Never claimed to mean anything to God." His head turned to the side of the bed all at once. "I'd like to be left alone."

Victor nodded and stepped toward the door. Jaycee followed after laying a hand on Caleb's foot.

The wind outside blew warm and whistling tunes.

CHAPTER 14

November 18th

Leigh lay in bed, barely aware that sunshine was now streaming in across her face. For the first time in recent memory, she had made it through the night without choking. She felt rested in a way she had forgotten she could be. She had half expected that when she slipped into sleep that she wouldn't wake up again, and now, realizing that she was still breathing, it felt as if her body pulsed with energy. For the first time in a long time, the pit in her stomach wasn't filled with anxiety; it was nurturing hope.

She slid out of bed gingerly, placing her feet gently on the floor. She had slept so well she hadn't even heard if Theo had come in, though if he had she didn't want to wake him. Deftly, she plucked the syringe and vial from her nightstand. The contents had felt like ice moving through her veins, and as she had slipped into sleep, she had felt the chill overtake her whole being. Now though, she felt as if a fire had awakened in her blood, giving her a will to live that she had sorely missed.

Leigh moved toward the window quietly, sliding the

pane open. A cool breeze cut through the slight fabric of her nightclothes, waking her up even more. Below, the alley sat in shadows, unoccupied. With grim satisfaction, she let the syringe and vial fall to the ground, to be obscured amongst the broken glass and refuse already littering the area. Content, she slid the window closed once more.

With deliberate strides, she crossed the room and opened the door to the en suite. The sun streaming through the window had warmed the tiles so that they felt pleasant against the soles of her feet.

She sat on the edge of the bath with her feet still firmly planted on the warm tiles for balance, and placed the stopper in the tub. Leigh grasped the hot water knob then and turned it to its highest setting before turning the cold water knob just a fraction. Steam wafted into the air, creating a pleasant haze of heat in the small room.

Leigh moved to the cabinet, taking out a stoppered bottle of lavender essence. The cork made a satisfying pop as she opened it, and by pouring it into the rising water the smell permeated the room. She inhaled deeply, feeling her airways open gently.

As the water continued to rise, she returned to the cabinet and extracted two plush white towels and laid them in the sunbeam streaming in through the window. She slipped her nightclothes off smoothly then, folding them tidily and placing them next to the towels before dipping her toe into the bathwater.

The heat was pleasant, and she let her whole foot sink in, stepping over the side of the tub and lowering her whole body into the water. She felt the calmest when she lost herself in the gentle lapping of water around her body. She felt as if she were one with the waves, as if she were part of that same unstoppable force that could carve out rock and sink ships as easily as it could quench thirst and give life to the land.

She let her head dip below the water, so used to holding her breath now that she barely noticed the transition. Her lungs did not ache now though, as they normally did when she woke at night drowning. Beneath the water she calmly watched as her hair swam around her head, black tendrils floating around her field of vision like ink.

She brought her face out of the water slowly then, and reached over to turn off the tap. Her hair clung to her scalp and neck like a cowl and small droplets of water hugged her cheeks, so that when the sunlight hit her face she seemed to sparkle in the light. The joy and peace she felt could not eclipse her sadness though. Despite her deepest wishes, she knew exactly what needed to be done.

CHAPTER 15

November 18th

Today is going to be awesome.

The words hang in front of Theo Flaherty like a promise. Like a sacrament. They stare at him in capital, bold letters on the big-screen HD retina display of his mind, each letter crystal clear and pixel perfect. The T is purple. The G and Y are yellow. All of the word 'awesome' is white and seems to glow, resonating from the page and shuttering from the pink rose hue behind it, a trick of the color wheel giving it a third dimension.

He blinks and shakes his hair out of his eyes, and suddenly the image fades into reality: no longer the crisp clean font of a digital billboard but something real and tactile in front of him. He can see the brush strokes on the pink, thick in some places and thin in others, and the badger-hair brush caught the paint in unclean, uneven amounts. It lifts and bends and flows in different directions: each stroke a declaration of intent upon the world made flesh. Behind the oblong matt of pink and flowers and celestial patterns, Earth and Sky combining in a series of cylindrical Kirby-esque dots of varied but complementary colors: orange, lilac, leaf green, fire red. The paint went on wet on wet, he instinctively knows. He can smell the paint thinner, used sparingly on the brush to fix mistakes. There are no mistakes here, just happy accidents. The words are carved into the paint after it dries, removing specific layers to reach the desired color underneath. The word 'awesome' makes it clear to the canvas below it all, down past even the primer coat. It is painstaking and arduous. The sweat of the painter is in it, their saliva, as their tongue sticks out the corner of their mouth and they lurch over the canvas, pressing gently but firmly into the layers of cornflower blue.

He was still on his bed but he could feel the whole house moving. There were men in white outside, each with their own chain strapped to their arms and hauling at the foundation of the building with all their might. It moved slowly – glacially – but they had all the time in the world, here. Change came slow, building for what seemed like a lifetime before exploding in huge, epistemic shifts.

"It's all a lie."

He sat up in his bed, his chest suddenly tight. His heart had grown fingers that were pushing their way out through the center of him, forcing his breast apart like an inside-out autopsy. He struggled for breath, his forehead immediately dotting with perspiration. The voice had come from outside his room; he'd know that as soon as he heard it. It was deep and authoritative and made him want to take off his mouth and scream. In his mind, he could bury his mouth into his fist like normal people would a pillow and suffocate it so that nobody else could hear, and scream as loud and as long as he wanted to, but that wouldn't make the feeling in his chest go away.

His chest was pounding, and he rose to his feet and stepped out his bedroom door.

All of the burners in the kitchen were on, glowing hot red and spewing heat up into the atmosphere of the room in great waves of distortion. The pots lay unsure on the counter next to them, filled to the brim with water that was just one degree above freezing. He swallowed hard and could feel his Adam's apple bulge. He paused at the stove and considered turning them off, then walked past them into his living room.

Chad Matthews was sitting on his couch, fiddling a deck of cards between his hands. The cards were stiff and new and Bicycle, Chad's favourite. Theo could smell the freshness of them from across the room.

Theo looked at his quizzically. "Did you?"

"Say that?" Chad finished for him, and then shook his head. "No, he's in there."

There was a door on the other side of the room that was closed tight; its stainless steel knob flaked with paint and wear.

Theo stared at it for a long moment. When he spoke to Chad again he was still eyeing it, his head turning toward his friend but his eyes refusing to tear themselves away. "Did you turn on the stove?"

"That's Abby."

He turned back and eyed the glowing spirals in his peripheral vision. They ignited the atmosphere around the stove in shimmering orange sparks, casting shadows on the walls of the kitchen in arcing patterns that reminded

Theo of Halloween. He watched them like that for a long moment, until his trance was broken by Chad's constant shuffling of the cards. His head turned as though mounted on a Lazy Susan under someone else's control, turning toward Chad but stopping short of him, centered on the room across the hall instead. The door across the hall loomed like a spectre, no light escaping from its edges, just bleeding darkness out into the rest of his apartment. He took a step forward toward it.

"Oh, I wouldn't do that," said Chad, still methodically shuffling his cards. He divided them into two even stacks and tapped them against each other to make them straight, then pressed his thumbs against their edges and flipped them until they were one stack again, repeating the process. He turned from his work to Theo and smiled. "Fifty-two times. That's what a study done by scientists at Harvard showed back in '93. For a deck of cards to be properly shuffled, you have to do this fifty-two times between deals."

"Seems like a lot of work."

Chad nodded. "Beat the odds though."

Theo took another step forward toward the door. There was something skittering behind it. He couldn't see it of course, only hear it: tiny feet moving one way and then the other, shuffling back and forth on nails that hadn't yet been cut and had grown back onto themselves. Teeth gnashed and saliva moved from one cheek to the other as it ran the circumference of the room over and over again, scraping the yellow paint off the walls at waist height all the way along. The room wasn't yellow actually, it was cappuccino brown, but he'd called it yellow. Leigh had said he was colour blind; he'd looked it up and found that it was an evolutionary trait: female saw color better, men saw shapes better. As such, he could see the shape of whatever was behind the door now, a lump with a rat-like head and large red eyes that never ever blinked. The hair on its back stood up on end and looked like spikes in the grease and sweat of its motion. Those gnashing teeth came down too long like its nails, coming down past its lower jaw and riding along the tile floor below it as it went. The pre-historic sabre-toothed mother-fucker.

There was a sharp pain in his neck and his muscles there tensed suddenly then loosened and finally melted. The melting feeling spread, irradiating outward from the spot where it had been, his arm going slack at his side almost immediately. His brain clashed against the base of his skull as though it was trying to escape through some heretofore-unknown emergency exit: Warning! Do not pass go. Do not collect two hundred dollars. He spun away from the door in an awkward lurch, but there was nothing there except Chad: still shuffling his cards but looking more and more worried.

"It wasn't me," he said defensively, the fear in his eyes contrasting with the ever-quickening pace of his shuffle. "It was him."

Theo turned in the direction he gestured. There was nothing there but the wall, his shadow cast upon it by the arcing orange sparks coming from the stovetop behind him. As he watched, his shadow on the wall moved independent of him, the bulges of his cheeks pushing upward in a smile as it raised its hand, revealing the hypodermic needle it held.

His left leg went numb to match his right and he stumbled, his cheek on that side sagging.

"I told you," Chad said, still shuffling his cards methodically.

Theo turned from the wall back to the door, which was suddenly and independently open. There was no black bedroom or rat-like beast though; instead, the door on the opposite side of his apartment opened to the clear, clear, sterile hallway of the Black Springs institute.

"No." He spoke the word not as a command, but as a plea.

He tried to back away, but the numbness that still spread throughout his body refused to comply. Suddenly his disobedient limbs lurched forward against his will and he was walking toward the door to Black Springs. Sweat beaded the patch of skin between his thin eyebrows as he tried to turn away and claw at the track that he was riding along, do anything to stop the way he was going, but he couldn't. His hips wouldn't move and his fingers would not clench. He slid back farther and father, his legs still stumbling forward no matter how hard he fought, unable to do anything except listen to Chad's constant shuffling of the cards.

He moved back until his back was perpendicular to the ceiling, and before he knew it he wasn't shuffling forward but was being wheeled on a gurney that he had been strapped to. Nurse Lachesis and Nurse Atropos appeared on either side of him, their faces aglow in the orange from the stovetop as they wheeled him through the hallways of Black Springs until they made it to the operating room, the ceiling of which had been painted bright and spectacular colors for the benefit of those going under. The brush strokes of the pink were thick in some places and thin in others, and the badger-hair brush caught the paint in unclean, uneven amounts. It lifted and bent and flowed in different directions, each stroke a declaration of intent upon the world made flesh. As his world went dark around the edges and he finally gave up on consciousness, he knew.

Today is going to be awesome.

Theo woke to a prod in his ribs, causing him to wince before he blearily opened his eyes. An officer stood over him, flashlight extended in front of her. "Sir, I'm going to have to ask you to get up," she said sternly, motioning for him to rise. He obliged, groggily.

"Sorry, officer, I didn't mean to fall asleep. I had just meant to sit down for a bit and have my dinner before heading home," he mumbled, rubbing his eyes. His hair was plastered to his cheek where he had used the takeout box for a pillow.

"And is there a reason you were out so late, sir? You weren't drinking, were you?" she asked, assessing him as he rose.

"Oh, God, no, sorry," Theo blurted out quickly. "I'm sure this doesn't look very good, but I swear it was an honest mistake. I just needed to get out of the apartment for a bit to give my girlfriend some space. She got some bad news about her health and needed some time alone. I meant to head back before too long. She must be worried sick by now."

The officer looked him up and down again, softening slightly. "Well, I'll let you get on your way with a warning this time. A park bench is no place to go falling asleep. You're lucky nothing happened. We keep this city as safe as possible, but it's still a dangerous place," she said.

"Thank you, officer. I really appreciate it. You have no idea," Theo said, hurriedly digging in his pockets for his cell phone. He pulled it out, only to discover there were in fact no missed calls or texts from Leigh. "I better be on my way," he said. "Looks like she's been trying to get a hold of me."

The officer nodded, and Theo turned and jogged out of the park. He was exhausted, but relieved he hadn't been woken by anyone else. He supposed he could have probably handled the average bum or tweaker trying to rob him, but he shuddered to think what would have happened if his wakeup call had been courtesy of one of his father's men.

He began to dial Leigh's cellphone, listening as it rang time and time again. No answer. He snorted, brows furrowed, hanging up and punching out a text to her quickly.

I have some errands to run. Be safe today.

He stopped, staring at the phone for a moment as he waited for a reply. Again, nothing. He felt a lump rise in his throat, and an old desire crept into his mind. He wished he had someone he could talk to about the whole situation. He didn't feel like he was being unreasonable, but the way Leigh was acting made him feel like a fool. He wished he had a friend to talk to. For a moment, he wanted to call Abby. He closed his eyes and pushed the idea aside though, and instead dialled for a car service.

CHAPTER 16

Black Springs, Fifth Floor
November 18th
Caleb hunched over the toilet in the small, cramped bathroom as his stomach urged and expelled another fistful of stomach contents. It ripped at him, the brown sinew tearing at his already raw throat.

His face was clammy with sweat; although he was very cold. White flecks dotted his mouth. His head lolled up from its place in the bowl and he eyed the red button that hung by the IV cord next to him, then turned away and threw up again. The vomit splash made it sound like more than it was.

He ran a hand over his scalp. The small bit of hair that clung around his ears came out in clumps. He stared at it, shocked for a moment, then dropped it into the toilet and flushed.

∞

Black Springs, Lobby
November 18th
The lobby of Black Springs was filled with the persis-

tent clacking of the secretary's typing echoing through the room; and the sound echoed inside of Theo's head, each thud hitting his brain like a sharp knife. He had smoothed out his suit and fixed his hair before returning, though he felt as if the bags under his eyes still gave away his troubled state of mind. The secretary sat primly behind her desk, gatekeeper to his task. Her hair was neatly pinned up, her pixie like ears exposed as she worked. She stared so intently at her monitor that she barely registered Theo's arrival at her desk.

Theo cleared his throat gently to alert her to his presence, though she didn't look up. "Hello there," he said, laying his hand on the top of the desk. She jumped in her chair, eyes wide as she registered that he was there.

"Mr. Haven, back again? I don't recall seeing you on the appointment list for today. Is everything alright?" she asked, hand splayed across her chest as she calmed herself. For the first time, Theo registered the name badge pinned at her breast.

"I'm sorry to startle you, Caroline. I was just hoping I could pop up and see Nurse Feinberg about my sister today. She's having some misgivings about her treatment and I was hoping to get some more advice on the matter," he said, forcing a smile.

He was sure she could sense his desperation despite the smile, but to his relief, she smiled sympathetically at him. "I'm sure we can manage that," she murmured, placing her hand on his to comfort him. "Just let me call up to the ward and make sure everything is clear for you to go up. It'll take a minute or two, so if you'd like you can take a seat while you wait."

Theo obliged, turning and walking the few paces to a group of armchairs surrounding a water feature. He smiled gratefully at her from across the room, watching her speak softly into her headset, but unable to hear her over the soft trickling of the water. The anxiety that worked its way through his body seemed to seep out of him, and he wished desperately that he could sink as deeply into sleep as he did into the chair.

His eyes fluttered shut for a moment, and he found himself fighting sleep. The antiseptic scent he had so long associated with Black Springs seemed to be replaced by the pleasant aroma of the salt sea and lemon verbena. He allowed his shoulders to relax, but forced his eyes open, following the trickling water as it washed down the wall.

Entranced like this, the next thing he felt was the gentle touch of the receptionist on his shoulder. "Nurse Feinberg will see you now, Mr. Haven. Your visitor's badge," she said, handing him the small plastic card.

Theo smiled at her and thanked her, rising from the chair and walking with her toward the elevator. Caroline pressed the up button gently, and smoothed the sleeve of his jacket in a comforting manner, smiling at him and then returned to her desk. As the doors opened and he stepped inside, he felt his deep seated anxieties about the place slipping away, replaced with the calming assurance that all his problems could be solved within these walls. He pressed the button for the fourth floor, and then leaned back against the wall of the elevator as it carried him toward his destination.

With a soft ding, the elevator came to a halt and the doors slid open. Theo made his way into the ward. The main room was full but peaceful, with patients working away at crossword puzzles and reading quietly. Nurse Feinberg stood with the other nurses at their station, chatting with them while they all worked. When she saw Theo, she smiled and excused herself from them, making her way to greet him.

"I don't see you for months on end, and now you're here two days in a row. I'd be happy if I didn't know it was only because you're in such a hard place," she said quietly, placing her arm around his shoulder and guiding him through her ward. "So what exactly seems to be the matter, Theo?" she asked.

"Leigh is refusing to take the medication. She's been burned too many times to trust the treatment without more information, but we're running out of time. I'm at a loss for what to do, and we need to leave town in a couple days or my father is going to rain Hell down on us," he confessed. "She needs help. I need help."

Nurse Feinberg nodded understandingly. "I hear you. It's a big leap of faith for her, I'm sure. You're not seeming to be at your best either though."

Theo sighed. "I'm honestly not, but I don't have enough time to worry about that right now. I just want to help her, and then hopefully everything else will sort itself out."

They neared Nurse Feinberg's office, but she paused to consider what Theo said. "You remember the girl from yesterday? Alice?" she asked, to which he nodded. "Well, she's had her fair share of problems too. She's only barely started her treatment, but I want you to see how much better she is now. I'm sure if you've got reason to have faith in us, you can get Leigh to come around too."

Theo sighed. "I guess so," he replied.

"Hey, breathe deep and try to let go of some of that stress. I'm not letting you out of here without a few pills to get you through the week. I recall when I first sent you to Port Haven that clonazepam worked well; how about we get you set up with a bit to last you until you can get out from your father's shadow?"

Reluctantly, Theo nodded, following Nurse Feinberg as she resumed walking, this time leading him past her office. They turned at the end of the hall, arriving at a set of double doors where Nurse Feinberg scanned her card-key. They opened with a hydraulic hum, and she led him through to the other side.

As the doors shut behind him, Theo took in the new surroundings. This ward seemed much newer than any he had been on before, and seemed quite secure, yet serene. Outside each door was a card reader, and unlike the ominous steel doors that filled the other areas in Black Springs, this ward was comprised primarily of frosted glass, with clear or frosted glass doors depending on the sensitivity of what lay behind them. It gave the area a clean, well-lit feeling, as light seemed to filter through the entire ward unimpeded.

Potted ferns were outside most doors, casting a warm green glow on the floor and glass around them. The same saltwater and lemon verbena scent that permeated the lobby danced through the hall here as well, comforting Theo.

The pair stopped outside one of the frosted glass doors, and Nurse Feinberg knocked gently, and then swiped her cardkey. A soft buzz signalled the door unlocking, and she pushed down gently on the handle to open the door. She motioned for Theo to follow her inside as she entered.

Inside the room sat three people, Alice, and two women that Theo didn't recognize. He nodded to them cordially, and Alice smiled pleasantly at him.

"I'm sorry to interrupt, Doctor Augustus. This is Thomas Haven, the young man who helped Alice yesterday. I wanted to show him how much better Alice is doing today. His sister is still a bit apprehensive about treatment, so I wanted to make sure he sees we're providing the best treatment possible," Nurse Feinberg said.

The woman farthest from Theo smiled. "No trouble, Roberta. I'm almost finished with Alice and Ms. Aaron anyway. Thomas, feel free to pull over that chair and join us," she said, welcoming Theo and motioning to a chair against the wall. He obliged, hauling it over awkwardly, and seating himself next to Alice as Nurse Feinberg ducked out of the room.

"I'm glad to see you up and about today," he said with a slight nod of his head.

"I'm much better now actually. I'm so glad you've stopped by. Thank you so much for your help yesterday," she replied. Her voice wavered a little, and Theo realized she looked much younger than he had thought she was the day before. Her sickness seemed to have aged her, but now, with a little more colour in her cheeks, he realized she couldn't be much older than her late teens.

Ms. Aaron regarded the two of them for a moment, and then turned to Doctor Augustus primly. "If there's nothing further to discuss, I'll actually head out myself now. Mr. Loveless will want an update on his daughter and I still have a few media outlets hounding me regarding the other day."

Doctor Augustus smiled at the woman. "Of course. Let Mr. Loveless know we will be continuing treatment and that we appreciate his consent and his patronage, as always," she said.

With that, Ms. Aaron rose from her seat. "Good day to you then," she said, though not without a slight sharpness to her tone. Theo watched her as she left the room, suddenly feeling as if she were familiar to him; but his train of thought was broken as Doctor Augustus broke the silence.

"So, Theo Flaherty, correct?" she asked, one eyebrow slightly raised. Theo's brows furrowed and the anxiety that had melted away amongst the lemon verbena crept back in all at once. Upon seeing this, she chuckled, a soft smile spreading across her face. "Don't look so worried. Your secret is safe within this room. Alice certainly won't tell, and neither will I. Nurse Feinberg filled me in on the whole situation yesterday. I take it your friend isn't responding well to the treatment though?" she asked.

"Oh," said Theo, calming slightly. "Um, not exactly. She's refused to take it. She's paranoid after all the things that have happened lately. I didn't know what else to do though, so I came back to talk to Nurse Feinberg again."

"Ah, understandable. Well, I hope this meeting puts your mind at ease at the very least," she said smiling and folding her hands together. Theo suddenly became aware of just how tired he was, and resented the energy it was taking to shut out the obtrusive thoughts of everyone around him.

"Alice here seems much better than yesterday. I hope with your help I can help Leigh achieve the same," he said, looking back and forth between both women and attempting a smile.

"Yes, she certainly is," Doctor Augustus said, the warm smile still plastered across her face. "We have her stabilized, which was much easier than I anticipated actually, and we're working to help her understand her gift, but I think you already knew that."

Theo's mouth opened slightly, his surprise at being called out evident. "So she does…" he trailed off.

"I can't seem to die," Alice responded, her words measured. "I've tried so many times. I've been depressed since my mother passed… but without it I probably wouldn't have known until I was a little old lady. Doctor Augustus is helping me get better though, and while I stay here, she'll be able to run some tests to see how my gift might be applied to help others. They've had me up in palliative care sometimes. It's weird though… you can't imagine what it's like, being around people who you know are going to die when you know that you can't."

Doctor Augustus smiled more widely now. "Alice and her family are quite generous. Her father is funding her treatment, but also much of our research. Who knows, perhaps if we can understand how Alice's gift works, we could delay the ravages of cancer or other diseases until we have better ways to treat them."

Theo's brow furrowed. "So if Leigh came in, would you be hoping she could further your research too in exchange for treatment; because we really don't have that long and I can't see her being okay with that," Theo stated.

Doctor Augustus shook her head sweetly. "Of course not. We wouldn't want her to do anything she wasn't okay with. If we can understand exactly how her own gift works though, we can devise a better treatment plan, one that might include some of the knowledge we're gaining from Alice's treatment for example. We're making breakthroughs everyday, but privacy is still paramount."

"I'm glad to hear that," Theo said, relaxing slightly. The rollercoaster of information and emotion was starting to get to him, though good news helped him keep it together.

"How about we schedule an appointment for tomorrow, same time, and Leigh can come in herself and figure out if this is what she wants to do? There's plenty of funding right now for us to treat her pro bono, and I'm sure we can put her worries to rest if we talk face to face," Doctor Augustus suggested.

"I can't guarantee she'll come in," Theo replied. "But I can't imagine a better option for her right now. You'll see me tomorrow for sure, and hopefully her too."

CHAPTER 17

Black Springs, Fifth Floor
November 18th

"I'm not sure when I find it hardest," said Ruben, facing the null space in the middle of the circle. Across from him, Nadiyah nodded. There was a small sore on her lip. "I mean, I always think I know, then some new thing comes up. I hate... I'd love to have a conversation that wasn't about cancer."

Everyone nodded.

"I never tried to keep it a secret. I never understood people that did before. I went home right after my diagnosis and told my wife and we both had a good cry, then we both told my kids and we all had a good cry... and I thought that was it. I thought it'd be like when they operated on my lung, you know: go to treatment, go to work, life goes on." He stopped and wiped nothing from his upper lip. It was sprinkled in thick gray hair that looked like straw. "It wasn't like that though. I don't know if it's the same for everything, or if it's *just* with cancer, but once you tell people, then *every* conversation is about the cancer. People look at you different, people talk to you different."

Lori nodded, so did a few of the others.

"It was the same for me," Hector said, his accent thick with bile. "After my first stroke I could still fight, but the other fighters they still looked at me different."

The nurse put a hand on his leg. "Ruben's talking now."

Hector nodded.

"There's this place where the cancer grows in conversation," Ruben continued. "These pregnant pauses. Like it doesn't just eat up your insides, it eats up the words people use with you, eats up their thoughts on you; it just eats and eats."

Caleb nodded and eyed the door, a tightness growing in his chest as the yellow piss dripped into his IV.

"And while I'm at it, I know this is horrible..."

"Not horrible," the nurse quietly interjected.

"... but I miss having sex. I used to love sex and I feel like that makes me some kind of pervert or something. I feel like I should have deeper concerns or some kind of bucket list of things I've never done, but all I want to do is something I've done a thousand times just one more time. I feel like that makes me weird. I feel like it makes me some kind of sex freak and I get so ashamed."

"It's not weird," Nadiyah said, speaking for the first time since the group convened.

"I assume it's not sex with just anyone?" Caleb asked, his voice hoarse. "But sex with your wife."

Ruben nodded.

"It's not even the sex then; you want to return to what

you loved most when you were well. There's nothing strange about that at all."

Ruben clacked his tongue against the inside of his upper lip, making a wet clammy sound. He stared at an unambiguous fleck on the floor for a moment, then looked up and met Caleb's eye. "You know what else is hard? You."

Caleb sat up straight, but did not respond.

"You being here like you are, it's cruel to the rest of us."

"Ruben –" the nurse started.

"I bet in every other ward in the state people can sit around and die and talk about it just like here. But they get to have faith. They get to have hope that there's something else waiting for them on the other side." His eyes welled up, but he did not cry, and his mouth distorted in rage. "I get to sit here and wish I could be with my wife like everyone else, but they get to tell themselves they're going to a place where that's all they'll do. That they'll get to do what they loved most during life all the time. You rob us of that. I'm not saying I had faith and I'm not saying I suddenly would have had faith, but with you here – you – I feel like I don't have the option."

"I'm so--" Caleb started.

"And don't say you're sorry. Just don't. Because I'd love to be able to go to some tent on the outskirts of town and have some faggoty little gimp put his hands on me and tell me I was healed, and I'd love to believe it. Even if it wasn't true, I'd love to just be able to believe it for a second. But with you here, I can't. Not with you sick."

There was silence in the room for a pregnant moment

in which nobody thought of cancer. Eventually Nurse Bethany moved on to someone else.

November 18th

Leigh stood staring at the outfit laid out on the bed for what felt like ages. The towel around her body was damp, and only the chill setting in on her skin propelled her to finally begin getting dressed. She moved toward the clothes tentatively, the whole act feeling far more symbolic to her than such a basic part of her routine would normally.

She had waited to leave her bath until the water was cold, and that same strain of procrastination ran through her actions now. She let her fingers flow over the smooth fabric of the tank top, but couldn't quite bring herself to lift it off the bed. Instead, she sat gingerly next to the clothes, staring at it a moment more.

Her phone buzzed on the nightstand, shaking her out of her trance, and she reached to get it. The message on the screen brought her fully back to reality, and without replying to it she replaced the phone facedown on the nightstand. More quickly now, with movements as smooth as smoke curling away from a flame, she rose and began to dress.

Her clothes clung to her like a second skin: forming to her curves, but still allowing her to move freely. Over the tank top and tight leggings, she shrugged on a black shawl, which billowed around her as she moved. In the warm fall sunlight flooding the bedroom, she looked like a swirl of ink dropped into crystalline waters.

A knock on the bedroom door startled her, and she

twirled around to face the direction of the noise. "Leigh," Theo called out. "Is it okay if I come in?"

She grimaced slightly, realizing that her delay getting ready meant that he had had enough time to return home. She forced herself to look neutral though, reaching and sliding her phone into her pocket and out of sight before replying. "Sure thing," she said.

Theo opened the door slowly; bringing an almost tangible nervous energy into the room with him. Her heart sunk looking at him, still wearing the clothes she had seen him in the day before and looking almost hollow for lack of sleep. She felt a desperate aching in her chest that things could go differently, or that she could avoid dragging him down any further. She knew what she had to do though.

"Hi," Theo started timidly. "I'm really sorry for the fight we had. I'm just trying my hardest to help, and I'm scared what's going to happen to you if I can't. I didn't mean to freak out."

Leigh looked him over, her face straight. She felt like she had defeated him, which was the last thing she wanted to do to him. Pity welled up in her throat. "You didn't freak out," she said. "I did. I'm scared too, but I was serious when I said it's not your job to help me get better." She paused, watching any glimmer of hope melt off his face. "Theo, you can't help me," she said coolly.

"What do you mean? I've done everything I can, and there are options for you if you're willing to see them. Please, just trust me," he pleaded, taking her hands in his.

She withdrew them, brow crumpled. "Theo, I'm leaving. This whole fling has been a mistake. You're a good guy, but I just don't love you, and I can't keep stringing you along into more and more trouble. Get out of town and get on with your life." She refused to look him in the eye as she said this.

Theo recoiled from her words. "You're lying," he said simply, pain deep in his eyes.

"I'm not. It's been a long time since I've had company or someone to care for me, but I think it's just been too long for me to remember how to care for someone back. I'm better alone and always have been," Leigh said.

"No, I know you're lying. I've seen inside your head enough to know how you've felt." Theo's voice turned hard now, anger and frustration creeping in. He grabbed the side of her face, forcing her to look at him. "Why are you doing this?"

"I'm doing this because it's how I feel now. I've thought long and hard about this. All I'll do by staying with you is hurt you," she spat, pulling away from his touch. She could tell by the look in his eyes that he had read her; that he knew she was telling the truth.

His hand dropped to his side limply, and he let out a long breath. "Fine then. Leave," he whispered; and then louder, with his voice growing bitter, he continued: "But don't forget you were the one that made this decision. They could've helped you at Black Springs. I could've helped you, if you would've let me. We could have tackled all of this together."

"I never asked for help," Leigh shot back.

"Here's the great thing about people who can read minds though, Leigh: you never had to ask. I could see you needed help, so I helped. Too bad I didn't see how much of a bitch you are," Theo spat.

Leigh didn't let it show how much it all hurt; she just focused on the task at hand and pushed her real feelings to the back of her mind, where even Theo wouldn't be able to get at them. She mustered as much ice as she could then, letting her words cut: "Well, I guess it's good this is the last you'll see of me then. Do yourself a favour, Theo. Don't find me again."

She pushed past him then, shutting the door firmly behind her and making her way out of the building down to the waiting car below.

Black Springs, Fifth Floor
November 18th

"Scat," Victor said, scooping up the cards scattered before them into his massive palm. He tapped them against the table twice and they all became uniform and even. He licked his thumb and began to deal them again, three each: Caleb Jaycee himself, Caleb Jaycee himself, Caleb Jaycee himself.

"Sounds like this guy is a real piece of work," Jaycee said, lifting the edges of his cards for only a moment.

"No, he's right," Caleb frowned, picking up his cards one at a time and then laying them side by side in front of him. They were evenly spaced, like a street vendor setting up to play Find-the-Lady. He picked a card from the deck and laid it back into the pile. "Or he's not wrong. I'm not sure that that automatically means right."

Victor gave Caleb a long, side-on glance. He smiled after a moment but said nothing, looking at his own cards.

"What, preachers aren't allowed to get sick?" Jaycee scoffed, picking from the pile and placing it in his hand. He threw away the queen of hearts. "Naw, he reminds me of this douchebag from back home, guy named Jackson Cooper. Just that type of mouth-breather that likes to blame everyone else for his problems. If it's not foreigners, then it's immigrants; if it's not immigrants, it's women; if it's not women, it's blacks; if it's not blacks, then it must have been that little fucker Jean-Claude Maximus. Can't have faith because you're here. Fuck him."

Victor picked up the queen of hearts and threw away the two of clubs.

Caleb picked a card from the deck, then threw it away again. "People say stupid things when they're scared and confused."

"You could have stopped that at people say stupid things," Jaycee said. He picked up the nine of clubs that Caleb threw away and discarded the jack of diamonds.

Victor picked from the deck. He looked at the four cards in his hand for a long time, running his tongue along the inside of his cheek. After a moment, he plucked the same card out of the lineup and threw it away. "Do you remember dreams much?" he said finally.

Jaycee turned toward him slowly. "You say the strangest things."

"I tend to," Caleb answered, taking a card from the deck and discarding it immediately. "At least I think I do."

"How do you fly in dreams?"

Caleb's eyes became distant for a moment, after which his eyebrows (or the curve where his eyebrows should have been) bobbed. "I guess I don't."

Jaycee picked up the five of spades and threw it away.

Victor picked from the deck. "Do you ever dream that you're someone else? And if you do, does it feel like you're someone else? Do you sit there and go 'wow, I'm Mitt Romney,' or are you just... them?" He threw away a different card, the three of hearts.

Caleb picked up a card and threw it away without really looking at it. "I can't say I've ever dreamed of being Mitt Romney."

"Mostly because we call those nightmares," Jaycee mumbled, throwing away the three of diamonds.

"But you do dream of being other people?" Victor pushed.

"I'd say so."

"Often?"

"Often enough."

Victor stared at him for a long moment, his gaze moving from Caleb's eyes to the bald area of his brow. "I had this friend once. We were walking together in the market – not what you'd call a market. Not something hipsters would go to. This was in-country. We were at the market and we were talking, kind of like this; I can't remember what about. We're walking and we see this kid, maybe fifteen years old, and he steals this bootleg action figure from a table. And I go to say something and my friend stops me. Now I get it, we've all heard the story of the little boy that steals bread to keep from going hungry, is he really a thief? But this was an action figure. Some kind of orange Power Ranger or something. So my friend stops me and he says, 'You can't judge the needs of other people based on your own needs.' That really stuck with me. A lot of what he said stuck with me, but that... that just stuck in there. I'll get pissed off sometimes and I'll remember that, and it'll just calm me down. It puts things in perspective."

Jaycee learned forward on his knuckles, listening.

Caleb maintained eye contact with him for a long moment, then nodded. "It sounds like your friend is very wise."

Victor nodded and smiled, just visible around the corners of his scruff. "He was."

"I take it you didn't go after the boy?"

Victor laughed in one giant sound from his diaphragm. "Ha, no. No, I don't think I ever saw the boy again. Or maybe I did; I had a hard time telling one from the other."

"So I guess the story ended happily."

Victor's smile slowly faded. "The shopkeeper heard us talking and assumed my friend had stolen the toy. He pulled a knife on us – and by knife, I mean a machete."

"Jesus," Jaycee breathed.

"He held it so close to my friend's pupil that the blade touched it, and he yelled and screamed something. Some of it was English, most of it wasn't. He wanted the figure back or he wanted the money for it, and we didn't have either. I'm getting ready to jump this guy, and my friend says again: 'Don't judge the needs of others based on your needs.'"

He licked his lips and picked up a card from the deck.

Jaycee stared at him, yellow-tinged eyes wide. "What happened?"

The smile pricked the sides of his mouth but did not return. "He said something to the man in Songhay – I guess that was the man's language, I could never tell those apart either. He would never tell me what he said and I wouldn't be able to repeat it if you paid me, but the shop keeper started to weep. This was a large man, and he just started to weep uncontrollably. He kneels on the ground and cries into the dust. I loosen up, and after a moment my friend puts a hand on the shop keeper's head... and the shop keeper screams, picks up his machete, and brings it down."

Both Jaycee and Caleb stared at him.

"Did he die?" Jaycee asked finally.

"Hnn? Oh, no. He lost a great deal of flesh off his arm and a toe, but he said he didn't use that much anyway. The weird thing is after the blow had been stuck he just stepped to the side, red blood soaking into his white shirt. I'd never seen him bleed before. It made me so mad. The shop keeper was in the dust again crying, and I picked up something from the table – I'm not sure what – and started hitting him with it. Whatever it was, it did the job very well. After a second my friend pushes me back, just enough to get me off the shop keeper, and I get his blood on me. I'll never forget that; his blood just all over me.

"He didn't speak to me for a week after that. No matter how many times I came around, he wouldn't see me. I was starting to think I'd really fucked up when I come home one day and find him just sitting at my table drinking kola tea. And he says it to me again, that we can't judge the needs of others by our needs. And I ask him why my needs were so different. If the shop keeper needed to take a pound of flesh, why couldn't I need to pound into his for it? He stands up and he looks down at me and he says, 'Because you're supposed to be better than that;' only he doesn't say that. What he says is: 'Did you need to do that?' And I couldn't even look at him. He never brought it up again."

Caleb smiled.

Victor looked down at the cards in his hand, and then laid them face-up on the table. They were the king, queen, and ace of hearts. "Scat. I think that's game."

Jaycee mucked his cards into the deck. "Wish Chad was here to show you up."

Caleb turned over his cards. He'd had three tens.

Victor pointed at it. "That's thirty and-a-half. You had that since the start of the hand."

"Why didn't you play with that? You would have won."

Caleb shrugged. "Guess I just thought I could do better."

Victor smiled.

CHAPTER 18

November 18th

Hale stared silently and intently at Leigh as they drove. She hadn't said a word since getting in the car, only nodded when he had asked if her arrival meant she was ready early. She looked much better now than she had at their last meeting, but her air of wellness was accompanied by a burning anger that certainly didn't seem to lack fuel.

He cleared his throat, causing Leigh's gaze to shift from the cars they were passing to him. She regarded him for a moment with a look of measured contempt, pulling her shawl tighter around her body. She looked as if she was about to turn away from him again when he spoke.

"We'll celebrate, shall we? You're looking marvellous and I can only imagine you're feeling even better," he said as he reached for a bottle from the pocket of the door.

"I won't have any," Leigh said firmly. "I just want to discuss the terms of our deal."

Hale smiled coldly. "You're nervous now, aren't you?" He sat up a little straighter in his seat. "You're wondering what we want you to sacrifice to keep yourself healthy."

Leigh didn't say anything for a moment, merely re-garded Hale's worn features. She hated his arrogance. She hated the position he had her in. "You're right," she said finally.

"Well, it's a good thing I'm so kind," he said, a satis-fied grin spreading across his face. Leigh hated his arro-gance. "Ms. Blackheart, all Circe wants is for you to re-sume the duties you had at Shane. Of course, it'll be on a bit of a larger scale, but I have a hunch you're good for it. You've already got enough pieces in place to start off quite well."

"What's that even supposed to mean?" Leigh asked darkly, shifting in her seat to better face him.

"You've had your hand in quite a few big gigs over the years; don't sell yourself short. You know the drill: there are plenty of things we want at Circe, plenty of informa-tion we need to obtain, people we need on our side. You've got a knack for getting your hands on things quietly, and that's all we want you to do for us now," Hale answered.

"So what, just your run-of-the-mill corporate espio-nage and head hunting? Isn't there someone less pricey you can get to do that for you?" Leigh asked, eyebrow raised.

"You know Circe doesn't want anything 'run-of-the-mill', Leigh. We're waist deep in this genetic war, and we need a better soldier in the fight. Shane has their weapons, and Engen has theirs; we need a weapon that can take on both of our enemies," Hale scoffed.

Leigh's heart sunk. "So what, I'm your new hit squad and thief all in one?"

"I didn't say that. You're a beautiful girl, Leigh. You're

charming, you're a smooth talker, and now we've worked out the kinks in your biggest flaw. You're endearing, and now you're practically unstoppable, so long as you continue this treatment. All those qualities are a recipe to bring in new recruits," Hale said, smiling once more. "We can create and trap as many gifted people as we like, but it's hard to gain the trust of people hiding in the world out there when you're a big military operation."

She had had her suspicions, but Hale's confirmation brought a small relief that she had done right by Theo. It was safer for everyone for her to have as few connections as possible. "I don't think I'll be nearly so much help as you hope," she murmured.

"Oh? From where I'm sitting you're sitting at the base of a very powerful tree," Hale said. "You've got that boyfriend of yours, Theo Flaherty; and we know for a fact that you're not the first gifted person he's come across. You shake that tree, and plenty of other resources will come tumbling out of the branches."

Leigh smiled sadly. "Too bad I've burned that bridge then," she said. "It's over between us."

Annoyance crept onto Hale's face as he scrutinized her features for the tell tale signs of a liar. Finding none, he sneered. "Maybe you're not as smart as I thought, ruining your best chance to survive."

Leigh looked at him and suppressed a laugh. "I'm my own best chance at survival. I always have been, always will be. Theo's hardly my only connection, and with his powers he would only be a liability to you anyway. You don't want him in your head."

Hale's face was still crumpled into a scowl. "Convince

me then."

November 18th

Theo lid in bed, staring at the ceiling and watching as the lights of passing cars drifted through his room. He felt a hollowness as his eyes followed the softly glowing beams, but he pushed the feeling aside as best he could. He didn't want to think about how quickly everything had fallen apart, or about what he could have said differently.

As soon as she had left, the anger had fallen away and he had been filled with regret. He hadn't meant to lash out at her. She had sparked his frustration though, the culmination of everything he had been through in the past few months; and in doing so she had received all of his anger. Everything from the time he had left Port Haven until now had been swirling in the pit of his stomach for so long, eating him up and weighing him down. It seemed like a mountain of inadequacies were piling up on him, and no matter how hard he tried the mountain kept growing.

Theo sighed, closing his eyes deliberately. He wanted nothing more than to wake up back in his dormitory and spend the day losing himself in swirled pigments. He wanted his dedication to mean something, to be able to express for once how he felt without outside noise pushing in on him.

The outside noise was getting louder lately, more static surrounding his own thoughts. Some days, it could be as dull as a radio left on low and tuned between two stations, but more and more it felt like his mind was hosting a whole crowd again. Helping Leigh had been enough of a distraction for him to block most of it out, but the more he tried, the harder it became.

Theo rolled onto his side, turning away from the window. The light from cars outside was streaming in, a mix of traffic and streetlights preventing him from sleeping, but he couldn't muster the energy to rise and close the drapes. As he settled on his side, he felt the hard form of a pill bottle dig into him, and he remembered the prescription Nurse Feinberg had filled for him.

It seemed like a reminder of his failure that he needed help just to keep it together. For a moment, he struggled with the self-loathing before rolling onto his back once more so that he could extract the bottle from his pocket. He held it above him, examining the label with heaviness in his chest, then unscrewed the lid and fished out a single pill. He popped it into his mouth, worked up saliva so that he could swallow it, and then choked the pill down.

He lay there for a while, listening to the hum of his neighbours' thoughts mixing in his head, before the pill began to take effect. Ever so slowly, the voices became quieter and duller, and Theo felt his heartbeat slow. He paid special attention to his breathing, following each inhale and exhale, and very soon he found himself slipping off to sleep.

CHAPTER 19

Black Springs, Fifth Floor

November 19th

Caleb lay back with his head on his pillow, staring up at the Van Gogh Wheat Field.

In the upper right quadrant there was a small red house, only the roof of which could be seen. It was long and bent in the center, as though still sunken from the previous winter's heavy snow. Around it there were elm trees that reached high into the sky with trunks barren of needles until they almost reached the roof, themselves victim of some strange ecological circumstance as well.

To the left of the house was a plume of smoke that rose up from the ground in a spinning thin tendril, expanding out near the top of its mark. He looked at that for some time; that blight on his scenic blue landscape tickling at the back of his mind.

His door opened and there was a familiar-but-painful sound of metal on metal that always accompanied Susan bringing in the food trolley. He smiled and sat up a little in his bed, then pulled the sheets taut so that there were no wrinkles.

"They didn't have rice cereal in the kitchen today, so I got some oat clusters. Now, I added some hot water and let it sit in the milk there for quite some time, so it should be soft enough that it doesn't give you any trouble digesting. I did get the cranberry juice you've been talking about, and there's some herbal tea there. I'm not sure if herbal tea is good for in the morning, but there's nothing saying you have to drink it in the morning; you can just lay it aside and have it whenever you want and there's enough there for if company comes over too."

She moved around the room in short spurts, to the trolley and back, to the trolley and back. There was something different about her. Caleb sat up straighter to try and see, but she moved very fast. "Susan," he said finally, raising his right hand.

She stopped and made eye contact with him, but said nothing.

She was wearing lipstick. Bright red lipstick that looked even brighter when framed against the yellows and blues of the wheat field. They became the small red house, the fixture of his attention for that long expectant moment.

He said nothing. He lowered his hand to the bed solemnly.

∞

Black Springs, Fifth Floor
November 19th

The group sat in a circle and stared out into the abyss of the circle, looking toward each other yet somehow never looking at each other. Like strangers on a crowded train that somehow all manage to avoid eye contact with each other, each of the five of them managed to be completely alone even in the small room.

There was no empty chair where Hector had once sat. As someone wheelchair-bound, he had always brought his own. This weighed on them collectively. There should have been an absence when a person left the world, but instead there was nothing. He left the world without leaving a fingerprint on the room, and somehow that hurt more than the leaving. The knowledge that the world was not different for his not being there, and might it be different for their not being there. They all felt this, but none of them said it.

Ruben was hunched into himself, staring at the floor beneath him. He was thinking of his wife, and how long it had been since he'd seen her. When he'd first been admitted into the palliative floor of Black Springs, she'd visited once a day, then once every two days, and now she stopped by when she could. His being there had become part of her routine, and in that way he had lived too long. Not for the first time he wondered if she had begun seeing someone else. He hoped that she had. He was unable to take care of himself, and he hoped dearly that she had found someone to take care of her. Watching a spouse die was a hard thing to do alone, he thought. He hoped she had found someone else, or that she would soon, but feared it all the same. He feared being replaced, of his absence leaving as little a mark on her life as Hector's chair had on their own.

Lori looked out the window at the wild blue beyond the clinic until she could see the swirls and swoops the wind made in it; or at least, she thought she could. She felt numb – the sort of still ash of feeling that settled over her and yet felt like nothing at all. She told herself it couldn't be shock; she'd experienced that before. She became obsessed and enamoured with naming this feeling. Regret? No. Shame? No. Sadness? That seemed simplest, but no. Whatever it was, it was not something she could assimilate to, something she could not even fully feel. The nameless emotion was like an iceberg: the majority of it submerged and unseen, but threatening to flip and cause great strife if one got too close.

Bethany stared at her clipboard full of notes and ways to start the conversation, but was so encumbered by which to chose that she chose neither and just regarded it with the blank stare of someone ill prepared for a test.

Nadiyah was crying. She was trying to keep herself quiet but found it hard, and every few minutes the sound would build and erupt out of her in a flow of sobs and gasps. She was thinking about Hector; in fact, she could think of nothing else. Her mind seemed to play his name on repeat, and every so often would spill out of her mouth along with one of the gasps and sobs and wails. She'd had the least experience with death. The only person in her life to die before she'd come to stay at Black Springs had been her grandmother, and that had been when she was six. She'd barely been able to process it then, and was making up for that now in spades. Since she'd come to the hospital, several people she'd known had died, and every time it had hit her like this.

Caleb stared at the floor. He thought about all of the times Hector had tried to talk to him. About the fact that they couldn't see the Hollywood sign. About the price of gas and just how much it was. About politics. About television. About women he'd fucked and women he hadn't fucked and women he still wanted to fuck. But more than anything about boxing. Hector Munez had loved to talk about boxing, and for the life of him Caleb could not recall the last time he had paid attention to him when he had. More often than not, he'd rolled away from him. He'd have walked away, were his legs anything resembling useful. He looked down at his legs now and hated them. If he'd been in front of a mirror and seen his reflection, he would have hated that too.

"He really was a boxer you know," he said finally. He looked up and made eye contact with Ruben, only because Ruben was who was sitting across from him. "I looked it up. He was a great boxer. He defended the middle weight title seven times."

Nadiyah started crying some more, in repeated and uncontrollable moans, then got up and left the room.

They all watched her go, then slowly let their heads drift back to being strangers on the train.

Caleb cursed, then pushed on his wheels forward and followed her.

∞

Black Springs, Fifth Floor
November 19th
He found her in the stairwell leading down to the fourth floor. She was curled into herself and crying, as though her center mass was a black hole pulling the rest of her in. She sat on the top stair and leaned against the wall, the stench of chlorine and pine everywhere. Her auburn

hair was in her eyes and stuck to her damp face, and her cheeks were marred by long trails of salty eyeliner. Her eyes were bloodshot and she shook. No matter how hard she tried, some part of her kept shaking. Her upper lip was damp with sweat and mucus that stung at the small open wound there.

Caleb wheeled his way over to her, wary of the stairs.

She turned and saw him and wailed uncontrollably when she tried to speak, eventually turning back toward the stairwell.

Fidgeting, he unbuckled himself and slid down off of his chair to be next to her on the stairs. He sat next to her and watched her cry for a long time, then reached out his right hand and took hers in it. Though his touch was soothing, she pulled away at first, then softened and let him hold her small, delicate hand.

"He was only sixty-five," she said, her voice watery with the tears she had somehow yet to shed. "I keep thinking that and it's so sad. My Nana was ten years older than that when she died and they still called it a shame, and yet here we are."

Caleb nodded. "Here we are."

She laughed despite herself. Her face seemed to glow. "I don't want to die," she said finally, followed by another long sting of sobs. "I mean, I know that goes without saying. I feel so stupid saying it. Nobody wants to die, not really. I know that everyone deserves it and that everyone wants more but I'm twenty-six. I mean you're supposed to be able to do stupid things when you're twenty-six. You're supposed to be able to do stupid things when you're twenty-four. You're definitely supposed to be able to when you're nineteen." She wiped her eyes. "I had this friend, Claire. When she turned twenty-six, she went swimming with sharks down in Cuba."

"Is she okay?"

Her chin wrinkled. "She's dead. It wasn't the sharks though, it was choices. Just stupid... stupid fucking choices."

He nodded again, and his eyes became far away. "Each of us owes a life."

She sobbed.

"Sometimes I feel like this has just dragged out. Sometimes – just sometimes – I feel like maybe I've lived too long. Like maybe there is some set number of years we have in us, a stamp that gets pressed into our foot as a child with a set number of days on it. Like a best before date." He was crying as well now. Not uncontrollably, just a few scant tears. "I'm starting to feel like I've gone beyond mine. It just feels like my best days are behind me. Like Hector. No matter how many years grew between, he spent all his years back in that ring. How could he not? With the lights and everyone just watching and cheering..." he paused for quite some time. "Like me with the tent. All my time, no matter how much I space I put between us, I haven't really lived since I was back in that tent." He clasped her hand tight. "Sometimes I'd give anything just to feel that one more time before the end. I thought back then I could take that thing anywhere... just pick it up and move it, and always face it East. But I can't carry it with me anymore. Somewhere along the road... it all gets left behind."

"I just want to have fun again. It's bad enough to

die. Everyone dies. But I mean, I could have gotten hit by a bus or fallen out a plane or gotten eaten by sharks and I wouldn't have to be around death all the time. The death… it's just here. It sits around in group and doesn't say anything and waits to look at you, and all you can do is wait." She sobbed again, and it became impossible for her to speak through it.

"You will," he said, patting her hand. After a long moment he added, "Have faith." It looked to physically hurt him to say it and yet was cathartic. At once, he sobbed and started to cry outright. He let go of her hand and buried his face in his palms and wept openly.

She hugged into him, and he hugged into her.

CHAPTER 20

November 19th

Theo sat on the gurney clutching his head in his hands, his nails digging into the back of his skull. He wanted to press them in deep and break the skin and peel back the veneer of his flesh until there was nothing left but the truth. His room was padded and sparse, devoid of any furniture save for his bed and a single Bicycle playing card on the floor directly in front of him: the three of hearts, face up toward the ceiling. It wasn't really the three of hearts though. No matter how long it kept up the charade, he knew that it couldn't be. His luck never changed, and he knew it.

"Theo?" Dr. Brakman said, leaning in with a smile full of teeth.

Theo blinked twice. His eyes hadn't been closed, yet somehow Brakman had just appeared in from of him where the three of hearts had been. He had known that the three wasn't really a three, but he hadn't thought it had been Brakman. If anything, he had thought the three was really a black ace, but now it was clearly Brakman:

He was sitting on the chair that was usually left just out-side his room. It was only brought in for Brakman. Any-one else who came in to talk to him had to stand or lean against the far wall.

Brakman was a short man with a large nose that came out of his face and tried to stab you when he spoke to you. He would always inch closer and closer when he talked, until there was nothing of your personal space left and your chest felt itchy and claustrophobic from it. He says his name like brac-MAN out loud and when people ask him how, but in his head it's BREAKman. Its on the bill-board he rolled in with him now, standing up behind him with spotlights shining up at it from every conceivable di-rection, blue letters on a bright green background: BREAK MAN.

Theo fidgeted, then squinted his eyes and turned away from the lights. His hands pawed and scratched at the base of his skull as if expecting to find some crease there that he could work his fingers into to finally reveal that he wasn't really Theo; there had been some mistake, a mix up at the hospital (that happened sometimes), and he was really supposed to be somewhere else. That they had the wrong man for this job. That he could just take off the mask and get away with it too (if it wasn't for those pesky kids and their dog).

All at once he looked up at Brakman, squinting with new knowledge. Pieces in his head started to come togeth-er, slowly at first and then with mounting speed. They moved like Tetris blocks, clearing away the lines of bullshit that had been made by years and years of wronged rights and righted wrongs.

"That's it," Brakman said, his voice as thick as honey but not sweet. He laid his clipboard aside and leaned forward, his face curled up. He was excited and threatening and happy all at the same time somehow. How could he be so many things at one time? "You're almost there."

Theo stopped clawing at the back of his scalp and brought his hands away spotted with blood. He wasn't wearing a mask; he knew that now (for the moment).

Brakman smiled at him.

Theo had seen the three and thought that it was supposed to be the ace of spades, but really it had been Brakman. But had the three really been Brakman? Or was the three pretending to be something else? Someone else?

He reached out and grabbed at Brakman's face. He made no move to stop Theo, and aside from a faint chuckle made no sound at all. Theo's fingers slipped past the rubber sockets of Brakman's eyeholes, his flesh becoming shaky and wrong like rubber.

Theo barred his teeth and pulled, Brakman's mask coming off all at once. It was Doctor Augustus underneath; her gallows smile still the same. The Ace of Spades in hiding all along.

CHAPTER 21

Black Springs, Fifth Floor

November 20th

Victor entered the room carrying a large brown paper bag. In it was a sandwich from the diner down the street that had been constructed by making a roast beef, spinach, onion, and Monterey jack cheese omelette that had been cooked to near-completion before being pressed between two slices of French toast and fried again. It was called the Om-le-GOD on the menu, and had lived up to the name the day before when he and Jaycee had had them. Jaycee was behind him, laughing at the tail end of the story of Mary's first time driving his old Ford pickup.

Caleb was sitting up in his bed with his table-tray positioned in front of himself like a desk. On the other side of the bed stood two people. One was Susan, who held her hands clasped before her stomach and looked like a wife from a fifties sitcom. The other was a tall, unknown man wearing a black suit and tie. He towered above Susan, his face gaunt and his cheeks sunken.

Caleb had a pen in his hand, and he clasped it with

some effort and intention.

"What's going on?" Victor asked, laying the sandwich down on the empty bed across from Caleb's.

"You shouldn't be in here," Susan said soothingly.

"The hell I shouldn't."

Jaycee's eyes went wide.

"It's okay," Caleb said, touching Susan's on the arm. "Really. I'm just taking care of some legal work."

Victor glared at him for a long moment, maintaining it as he walked out to the table and spun the paper to face him. It was deceptively short, for what it was, only a single page. "This is a DNR."

The words hung in the room like men sent to the gallows.

"It is," Caleb nodded, motioning for the paper to be put back.

"Have you lost your mind?" he almost yelled. He had wanted to yell and had started to yell, but had pulled back at the last instant.

"Victor," Jaycee said sternly, stepping forward.

Victor either ignored or did not hear him. "At your age, a DNR is unreasonable. It is unethical. It is... it is wrong. You cannot be serious about this."

"Victor."

"It's fine," Caleb said again, moving to sign the paper.

Victor moved it aside. He looked from Susan to the tall man and then back again. "And you, just sitting there all mousy. Is this what you went through medical school for? I thought nurses wanted to save lives. How can you sit there and care and *say nothing*?" Susan stepped back a pace. "Open your gob and tell him. Tell him how you feel. Lie to him, tell him the truth, tell him anything to get that pen out of his hand." He turned to the tall man. "And you, just standing there presiding over this. I've never seen such apathy, and if you knew what I'd seen you'd know to be offended by that. It's just a job to you. You should go back to smoking pot in your grandmother's basement and stop thinking about how you'd look in that nurse's outfit you --"

"Victor!" Jaycee bellowed, grabbing him by the arm and spinning him around.

For an instant it looked as though Victor might say something to Jaycee as well, but his face softened and slowly the redness drained from it and went back to normal. He straightened his shirt and turned back to Caleb.

"Do not judge my needs based on your own," Caleb said, softly.

The words hit Victor like a punch to the abdomen. He stood stunned for a moment with his jaw slack and watched, trying to come up with the words to rebuke the statement and finding none. As his train of thought crumbled before him, he stiffened and righted himself. His hands shook. "I apologize."

"It's okay," Caleb nodded, waving the apology aside with one motion of his hand.

"No, it isn't," he said again. He looked at Susan and the lawyer and nodded to both. Reluctantly he laid the Do Not Resuscitate form back on the table-tray. "Forgive me."

Caleb signed it and the lawyer snatched it away before Victor could take it again, sliding it into his accordion briefcase.

Victor stared at the case, then turned to leave. Jaycee followed him.

∞

Lacey's diner was small. It sat on the corner of Linegar and Grandview three blocks from Black Springs Clinic and five blocks from the motel Victor and Jaycee had been staying at. The El Dorado was parked out front and caught the sunlight in its windshield, reflecting it back into the diner.

Jaycee stared at Victor expectantly. His three-fingered hands were laced together and he watched the man across the table from him from over them. Victor's eyes were blank, like a man defeated. They both had coffee in front of them. Victor had ordered his 'correcto' and the waitress had given him a hairy eyebrow. From behind him, Jaycee had shaken his head at her and she'd given it to him straight. In any event, both cups sat in from of them full and doing nothing but producing steam.

"I don't get it," Jaycee said finally. He opened his hands and mimed strangling Victor, then brought them together again. "I don't get how you think. I mean, I get it. At least he makes sense, in a sort of strange video-game logic way. I never understood why I was on the team. You say I have potential; I don't see it, whatever. But Caleb, I get it. If you're playing an RPG you need a healer on the team."

Victor scrunched his nose and shook his head. He looked somewhere between confused and angry. "What?"

"I'm saying I get it. But I mean, he's on death's door

anyway. People do not come back from palliative care, Victor. He's not... he's not going to be any use on the team. He's never going to be on the team. I don't even know what the team is really for, but unless what we're for is hanging around a clinic, I don't see him being much use. I think you're wasting your time. And if you think that DNR is going to make that big a difference... I'm sorry, sometimes it's not a matter of DO not resuscitate, it's a matter of CAN not resuscitate."

"I'm not here recruiting."

Jaycee's hands flopped to the table and he gave Victor a deadpan expression. "Pull the other one."

"I'm not, I..." he massaged the bridge of his nose. He stayed like that for over a minute. Jaycee sat up, surprised at the effect his words had had. Victor took a sip of his coffee, and then spoke again: "Do you remember that story I told? About my friend in the market?"

Jaycee nodded.

"He had this way of thinking about the world and our place in it. He believed in balance and order and was just so good at it. Some of us have to try to be good men, for him he just... was. It wasn't a choice for him, there was no other option. The wrong thing just never occurred to him. He'd argue that of course, but he couldn't fool me. Not on that anyway."

Jaycee strung his fingers back together and leaned forward to listen.

"He thought the world was right as it was. It really shattered what I had in my head at the time... all this manifest destiny one-voice. He wasn't naive to the problems of the world and he didn't ignore them, but he thought that people, at their core, were good."

He took a long gulp of his coffee and smiled. His eyes looked damp.

"I'll never forget when I met him. I'd been dropped in Nigeria. The paperwork had said we were going in-country, but what our paperwork said and what the upstairs paperwork said didn't always match up. They sent twelve of us in and after three weeks there was just me left. No ammo and thirty pounds lighter than when I'd started. I came across this quaint little village and it looked like so much twigs and mud at the time. I got it in my head that I'd take it on my own. I could stay there and set up camp, they had to have food and water. I walked into the middle of town with my gun that only I knew wasn't loaded and there he was." He sipped his coffee again. "I hadn't seen a white man in weeks and yet here he was, as pale as a vampire while he sat out in the Nigerian sun with hair so blonde it was white and wearing white – everyone wore white, but he just stuck out. He just sat there, kneeling Indian-style and turned around and smiled at me. I was holding a gun to him and he waves me over and gives me some chicken. I ate it all, so he gave me some more. And while I ate, he was just talking and what he said made *no sense*... until it all started to make sense. Once he started to make sense, *everything* started to make sense. Before I knew it, my hair had grown long and I was what they used to call a Contentious Objector."

Jaycee still watched him, his eyes wide and eager.

Victor's eyes got sad. "He died alone. He was my friend – more than that, really – and when his time came, he died alone. I wasn't there, but I was told he fought right to the end to cling on... that was a thing with him. He valued *life* more than anything else. He never would have laid down or signed any DNR or done anything of the like. I have never taken up that gun or any other to take a life since. It's not what he would have wanted. It's not what I want. Life has meaning, it --" He stopped and looked at Jaycee, then lowered his hands. "Anyway, I heard about the boy and I just... something about him reminded me of him. Call it Buddhist folly."

"You're not Buddhist."

He laughed, and it fought back the tears until they were gone. He smiled at Jaycee. "I didn't want this person – Caleb – to die alone."

Jaycee nodded. He raised his hand to the waitress and ordered pie.

CHAPTER 22

November 20th

Theo woke slowly, the sound of car horns filtering in through the window along with the afternoon sunlight. He hadn't heard his usual alarm go off on his phone, but the rejuvenated feeling that usually followed such a long sleep hadn't graced his body. He lay still for a moment, assessing the aches and pains radiating through his joints, questioning where they had come from. The fog of sleep began to slip off him though and with it so too did the memory of his dream, although the shadows of fear still gripped at him.

He rolled slowly out of bed, feeling like an old man as his muscles struggled. He hadn't felt so weak since he had first arrived at Port Haven and had begun to practice sparring. His flesh felt tender, and he felt almost bruised, though only goose bumps marred his bare skin.

Moving gingerly, he dressed as quickly as he could, though he lacked the energy to make an effort with his appearance. Instead, he threw on loose linen trousers and a soft white t-shirt, sliding his feet into loafers and grabbing his wallet as he headed for the door. He felt a careless ease float over him, smothering the nauseating unease he had felt waking up. The paranoia that kept him sharp, that typically prompted him to double check the door as he locked it on his way out, seemed to have melted away courtesy of the clonazepam pumping through his veins. He barely noticed his door lazily swing shut behind him as he moved toward the elevator at the far end of the hall.

The chiming elevator doors only faintly rang out in Theo's ears as he shuffled into the suspended metal box. The braille on the button for the ground floor hardly registered under his fingertips, and as the elevator lurched to life he had the sudden sensation that his head was floating independently above his body. That feeling disappeared however, as the doors slid open and Theo's feet clumsily attempted to compensate for his altered state of mind. He caught himself abruptly on the trashcan just outside the doors, seconds from crashing to the floor and splitting his lip open on the worn lobby carpeting.

He picked himself up carefully, giving his head time to adjust to the change in height. Theo tread carefully, feeling as if he was walking through a pool of water. In the time it took him to reach the door, the world seemed to almost stand still. The whole world seemed so heavy to him that opening the door was startling, his overestimation of the strength needed to move it causing him to stumble backward.

His feet feeling like lead bricks, Theo moved onto the sidewalk and toward the road, hand outstretched to hail a cab. The yellow metallic body slid gracefully toward him, gliding in toward the curb in front of him. Theo waved languidly at the driver, as much effort as he could muster, and opened the passenger door so that he could seat himself. He barely registered telling the man where he wanted to go, but evidently he managed, because after winding their way out of the neighbourhood and onto the freeway, Theo began to recognize the roads leading to Black Springs.

Something buried in his mind screamed at him, getting louder and louder the closer they got. It remained cloaked in the heavy fog of medication though, the pill from the night before hitting him hard after being absent from his system for so long. He could vaguely recall it having been a similar experience the first day or so when he had begun medication before, but the feeling of relief he had once felt at the world slipping into silence in his mind was replaced with a masked uneasiness. A small part of him recognized the distinct lack of anxiety he was feeling, but rather than welcome it as a comfort, alarm bells seemed to sound in his mind. The forceful docility seemed a physical presence weighing itself on his chest.

Breathily, Theo managed to get out the words, "Do you mind if I open the window," to which the driver nodded silently, shooting him a glance out of the side of his eye. The cabbie's skin was darkened, leathery, and wrinkled from the California sun, but he seemed to pale a little weighing Theo's destination and countenance in his mind. Theo pressed the button for the window hard, sending it as far down as it would go. The cool fall air hit him in the face, sharpening his thoughts marginally.

His hair whirled around his head, giving him the sensation of being caught in the eye of a storm. The small details escaped him, but familiar road signs began to stick out to him. The crisp smell of fall air mixed with the sunshine beating down, but nausea curdled in his stomach.

As the car rounded the final bend, Theo felt bile rise in his throat. It blotted out the artificial relaxation gripping him, and he felt old emotions return. He felt a cold sweat on his brow as the car slowed to a stop in front of the lobby doors.

"Eighty-three," the cabbie croaked. "You payin' cash or credit?"

Theo sat stunned for a moment, the sudden voice after the absence of conversation confusing to him.

"Well boy?" the cabbie asked, a mixture of nervousness thrown into his gruff growl.

"Sorry," Theo stuttered. "Credit," he said, pulling out a card.

The cabbie retrieved a keypad without taking his eyes off Theo and rang the charge through. A small receipt curled out of the machine, and the man handed it to Theo with his card. "You have a good day now," the cabbie said.

"You too," Theo mumbled, clambering out of the taxi and leaning on the door to steady himself. He shut the door with more force than he intended, wincing slightly at the slam. The taxi driver barely waited a second once the door was shut to peel out of the lot however, leaving Theo slightly shell-shocked on the steps of Black Springs.

Theo hauled himself into the lobby, which seemed to him much louder than his last few visits, and made his way for the front desk. Caroline glanced up as he arrived, smiling. This time, he didn't have the energy to return the gesture.

"Mr. Haven, good to see you. Shall I page Doctor Augustus and let her know you're on your way up?"

Theo nodded. "Please."

The secretary's fingers danced across the keyboard in front of her. "I take it your sister couldn't make it today as well? There's a note on the file that the two of you were expected today."

"She decided to weigh her options, regrettably," Theo replied, attempting to keep up the façade with the woman.

Caroline smiled tightly this time. "Understandable. I hope she's well at least."

"Me too," Theo replied. He hesitated for a moment, unsure what else to say to the woman. "Thank you, you know, for everything over the past few days," he said, his tongue tripping over the words.

"It's been my pleasure," Caroline replied, her features softening to a small sympathetic frown. She handed him his visitor cardkey over the desk. "Take care."

Theo nodded curtly in response, grasping the card with his thumb and forefinger as he headed toward the elevator. He had tried to push aside Leigh's absence, had tried to ignore his reason for returning to Black Springs, but Caroline's question had brought Leigh's rejection back to the forefront of his mind. He thumbed the up button on the elevator with more force than necessary, a small burst of his anger and despair inflicted on metal.

The doors slid open in front of him almost instantly and he stepped inside, jamming his finger against the button for the fourth floor. As he did so, a twinge of pain shot through his temples and sent him to the floor. He let out a gasp as the elevator doors closed, clutching at his head. When the wave of pain subsided, spots danced dizzyingly in front of his eyes. The smell of burnt hair filled his nose, though there was no source for the odour. His skin felt as if it had an electric charge, like a current was swimming over it. All the fine baby hairs over his body seemed to stand on end, prickling ominously.

Theo pulled himself back to his feet, grasping at the elevator wall for support. The noise that had beaten down on him in the lobby seemed even louder now, though it was no more discernable now than it had been at first. It seemed to Theo as if a crowd hummed and cackled, drowning out sane thought with a thunderous voice. As the elevator lurched to a halt, he stumbled slightly, catching himself just as the doors opened.

He moved into the ward as quickly as he could, swiping the cardkey and passing through the door to arrive at the nurses' station beyond. Nurse Lachesis pored over a patient chart on a clipboard as he approached, but glanced up as he drew nearer. She seemed to size him up, brow furrowing as she cast her eyes up and down the length of him. Her gaze seemed to evaluate his every movement, fuelling feelings of paranoia with his every step.

"Back again, Mr. Haven?" Nurse Lachesis asked, placing the clipboard out of view on the desk behind her.

"Yes, I'm just here for the appointment I have with Doctor Augustus," Theo replied, surveying the room. It was practically empty now, and felt chillier despite the sun pouring in through the windows. He shivered slightly, aware for the first time that he had forgotten a jacket.

Nurse Lachesis seemed to smirk at his discomfort, but Theo discounted his suspicion as an accompaniment to his headache. "I'll escort you to her office then."

She linked arms with Theo, supporting him as she led him down the hall he had passed through the day before. The smell of burnt hair still clung to the inside of his nose, and as they drew closer to Doctor Augustus' office the lemon verbena aroma that had been so soothing the day before was nowhere to be found.

Nurse Lachesis was silent on their journey, guiding and supporting Theo as they passed down the halls. The thrum in his mind continued to swell, and every so often it sent flashes of searing red or white in front of his eyes, and the occasional screeching sound caused him to wince. For her part, Nurse Lachesis didn't mention his turmoil, though she surveyed him from the corner of her eye. Theo felt the acid in the pit of his stomach swell, and he worried that he saw amusement lurking in her features.

Finally, passing through security point after security point, they reached Doctor Augustus' office. The wailing in Theo's mind seemed to be climbing toward a dizzying peak when he finally recognized it for what it was. Certain voices seemed to grow louder in the frenzy, standing out like the caw of crows over a humming hive of bees. With horrifying surety, the realization struck Theo that he had let his guard down in the worst way.

He barely noticed as Nurse Lachesis guided him down into the chair across from Doctor Augustus and left the two of them alone in the room together. The woman sitting across from him seemed to be so much more than she had before, as if she were the queen in a nest of hornets.

They sat across from each other in silence for a moment, Doctor Augustus' hands folded and her eyes sharp as Theo tried desperately to close his mind. He felt like a caged animal, lured in with sweet honey only to find himself caught in a claw.

Doctor Augustus smiled as if to break the tension, but without warmth in her face it only felt sinister. "I'm sorry you're here alone today, Theo. I really had hoped Leigh would be joining us today."

"Unfortunately not," Theo said breathily, grasping the armrest of his chair with such force his knuckles turned white.

"You don't look too well yourself today. I imagine you're feeling the side effects of the new prescription pretty strongly," Doctor Augustus said.

"Yeah, nothing I can't handle though," Theo replied, gritting his teeth. It felt like he needed double the effort to close the floodgates on the thoughts intruding in his mind, something he could only remember happening in his earliest days at Black Springs.

Doctor Augustus surveyed his face like a card player looking for a bluff. "Are you so sure about that? Are you sure you're able to leave here today? We've always got a place for you here if you need it," she said empathetically.

"I'm sure I'll be on my way out shortly. I've got people waiting for me," he lied. "I can't be long."

Doctor Augustus relaxed in her chair. "Is that so? Roberta was so sure we were the only people you and Leigh could turn to."

Theo grimaced. "Yeah, well, I've got my own friends

to fall back on when I need them, and Leigh does too evidently," he said bitterly.

Across from him, Doctor Augustus' eyes sparkled and her brow furrowed, a small smirk creeping onto her face. "Your attempts to convince her to come in for treatment went that well?"

"Yep," Theo replied bluntly, staring into Doctor Augustus' eyes. There was no denying he carried a lot of baggage concerning trust issues with doctors and this very hospital, but she had seemed better. Now, he couldn't be sure. "I didn't see Alice today," he said. "Is she still improving?"

Doctor Augustus tutted. "Theo, doctor patient confidentiality prevents me from telling you that, you know that."

Theo glowered. "You didn't have a problem with that yesterday, when you had her around trying to convince me that Black Springs had turned itself around."

Doctor Augustus' smile turned sour as she replied. "I can assure you, Black Springs is very different from when you were a patient here."

"Yeah, well, at least when I was a patient here I could trust Nurse Feinberg to look out for me and make sure my medications weren't messing me up."

"I think you'll find Nurse Feinberg's got a ward full of people to take care of lately, and that little flock of hers has become her main priority," Doctor Augustus said coldly.

"So what," Theo retorted. "She didn't have the time to tell you what medication might mess me up?"

Doctor Augustus smiled. "No, she certainly did."

Theo felt a pit form in his stomach. "I'm leaving," he

said quietly.

A hush fell over the room as both individuals rose from their seats slowly. "You should know, I had hoped to help both of you, but it's hardly worth it for me to pursue you without her. You're nothing special these days, Theo," Doctor Augustus said.

"Well, I guess that works out well for me then," Theo replied darkly. He backed away from her, almost tripping over his chair.

"Do yourself a favour, Theo. I could easily get you committed. Take your father's advice, get out of town, and never look back."

Theo looked at her appalled. "Whatever happened to the Hippocratic oath? Do you just throw that out the window when you have an opportunity to line your pockets?"

Doctor Augustus chuckled a little. "It's never been about money for me. It's about being at the forefront of this new age. A little research and I'll be unlocking the next human frontier. Just you wait and see."

"Not with my help," Theo spat, yanking open the door to her office.

CHAPTER 23

Black Springs, Fifth Floor

November 20th

The room was dark, lit only by the light that came in around the edges of door. The effect on the Van Gogh was striking. Somehow it was night even in the world of the Wheat Field, the darkness making the blue of the sky look dark and foreboding. Only the wheat was clearly discernible, its bright sun-shiny haze turned to a dark golden mustard.

Victor sat on the edge of the bed, the light catching in his hair. Jaycee was behind him. He had taken his shirt off, unable to stand the heat of Los Angeles any longer, even in the night.

Caleb lay in the bed. His skin had turned a shade of dark green in his face and his extremities were yellow and bruised. His breaths were even longer and more laboured now. He'd been hooked up to a machine to help him take breath and could not leave the bed.

He had taken a turn for the worse quickly. His white cell count had fallen and his immune system was not responding with more. It had been the effect of total irradiation, without the radiation, Bethany had said. Victor had heard another doctor, named Brakman, shrug and comment that sometimes the body just gave up... but Victor knew that was a mask. He was just as confused as everyone else.

Victor reached out and gripped Caleb's hand, clutching it tightly. They locked eyes as though caught in a battle of wills, as Victor tried to force him to live. To somehow push his life through his arm and out into Caleb's.

"You should be fighting this," Victor said, his voice hoarse. His head shook as he spoke.

"I am fighting this," Caleb smiled. His teeth looked yellow. "I'm just not winning."

Victor reached to hold his other hand, but Caleb slid it away. "Life is important. Your life is important, not matter what state it's in or not matter how much time is left. I almost died once, years back... the years since, I don't know what I would be without them. Because I let someone help me."

"You wouldn't have missed them," Caleb laughed, then coughed. "You'd have been dead."

"You won't let them help you. You helped so many people, how can you deny other people that feeling. This is... this is selfish. This is selfish and obscene and... you have to have faith in other people, the way they had faith in you. You could do so much more."

He smiled. "I'll leave that to you."

Victor lay his head down. He made no sound for several long, agonizing minutes. Jaycee reached out only once to place a hand on his back, then thought better of it.

Victor kissed Caleb's hand and looked up, his face wet.

"You know I'm right."

"I know you're sure. I know you're not right, not this time."

Caleb allowed his gaze to fall past Victor to Jaycee, and then past Jaycee to the Wheat Field. "Perhaps maturity and knowledge aren't measured by the amount of time we've been here, but the amount of time we have left." He allowed his gaze to fall back to Victor. "At which point, I hope you don't understand for a long, long time."

Jaycee stepped over and took Caleb's left hand, cupping it in both of his. He turned his head down and it became dark and gray.

Victor wept.

Susan came into Caleb's room pushing her trolley. It made its familiar clanging sound as it popped over the divider between the hall and the room. "It's your choice on the menu today," she said with ironed-on cheer. "We've got the regular assortment, but we can cook you up anything you want, if you're up for it; so whatever you want I can get."

Caleb raised his hand for her to stop, and she did. Stopping the act seemed to upset her, as though the pretending had not just been for him.

"You've been beautiful," he said, his voice almost a whisper.

"Thank you."

"Wear your lipstick for me tomorrow."

Her mouth opened. She closed it, smiled, and nodded.

CHAPTER 24

November 20th

The lights were bright all around her.

Alice kept her eyes shut firm, but she couldn't block out the sounds assaulting her ears. The other rooms along the hall echoed with wailing and moaning, creating a cacophonous clash in her head. The thin skin of her eyelids kept out the worst of what was around her, but the irritating flash of the red lights on her monitoring equipment burned through to light up the dark world in her head. She could hear the occasional screech of metal through her door as well as the squeal of wheels rolling down the hall.

Her cheeks stung a little, the salt from dried tears irritating her skin, and her hair scratched and itched at her neck. She longed to brush it out, to flick it off her skin or pile it up into a ponytail, but the straps around her wrists cut into her arms when she made the slightest movement. The same was true of the ones around her ankles, which seemed to chew hungrily into her flesh.

The door creaked open ominously, Alice's eyes shooting open and darting around. They rested finally on the young nurse who had entered the room, brown hair cascading down her back. She stood back on to Alice at the foot of her bed, poring over a clipboard. As she scanned the last page and flipped back to the front, she began to turn toward Alice. The girl shut her eyes quickly, attempting to make her breaths even and slow to feign sleep.

Alice listened as the nurse's footsteps drew close to the head of her bed, stopping. She imagined the woman surveying her, though she feared what for. The discord echoing in the hall outside still filtered into the room, and Alice felt as if she would be smothered by it.

"It won't be long now until things get interesting," Nurse Clotho whispered. "I know you're afraid, and that's good, it's perfectly normal. Just hang in there, and I promise you'll be pleasantly surprised at how things turn out." The woman's voice was quite and almost comforting, and as she spoke, she gently brushed Alice's hair off her neck.

The lights were still bright all around her, and the red flash stung her retina. In her mind, she screamed.

CHAPTER 25

Black Springs, Fifth Floor

November 21st

Victor stood by Caleb's bed with Jaycee behind him as ever.

"Take the painting," Caleb said, holding an oxygen mask to his face.

Victor turned and regarded the Van Gogh from where it hung on the wall. "I couldn't."

"Take it," Caleb rasped. "It has often soothed me and brought me joy. Something about it just seems like... happier times. Like old friends."

Victor nodded. "I understand."

"You seem like a well travelled man. Have you ever been to a place like that? Where there's nothing but fields of yellow growing sun?"

"I have."

"I have been there many times in my dreams. I walk with friends and I'm so happy, Victor. The tips of the wheat kiss my fingers and there's nowhere I'd rather be than right there at that time and place."

Victor nodded. "I feel the same way, often."

Caleb smiled. Then his smile faded and he turned toward the window. "I think I should like to go there, now."

Victor pursed his lips and nodded once. He turned to the beeping machine beside the bed, lifted the plastic guard, and switched it off. He held Caleb's arm straight and gripped the IV that fed into it, the liquid in the bag having long since been switched out from urine yellow to the calming clear of morphine.

Jaycee laid a heavy hand on Victor's.

Victor turned and looked at him. "No. You don't need to do this."

"I don't need to," Jaycee agreed. "But you need not to." He held Victor's gaze until he released his grip on the cord. "I know why I belong on the team, now."

Victor nodded.

Slowly Jaycee pushed back the dial on the IV until it was at its maximum. He gripped the cord with both hands and knotted it, kinking the vine firmly. The clear liquid pooled for several long minutes and Caleb's breath began to labor, when Jaycee let the cord go. He stepped back and joined Victor and they both watched.

Some time later, he stepped forward again and removed the IV from Caleb's arm. He pressed his callused thumb to the place where it had been to stop the blood flow, but found that there was none. He nodded, then turned out the light.

CHAPTER 26

Black Springs, Fourth Floor

November 21st

Theo had broken into a run the minute the door shut behind him. He skidded to a stop now though, reaching the mouth of the hallway filtering back into the psych ward lobby. Clustered around the nurses' station, Atropos, Lachesis, and Clotho seemed invested in whatever work they were engaged in. Worry set in as he realized they stood between him and the door to the elevators. Had Doctor Augustus sent people to stop him leaving? He was too afraid to open his mind up again to find out if she had.

In the seconds he stood there debating what to do though, the faint screeching and wailing he had heard reverberating in his head started anew. The three women's heads shot up in unison, eyes searching down the corridor closest to them, and Theo realized this time the noise wasn't just in his head.

"Should we go check on them again?" Nurse Lachesis asked.

"No one is going to die today, you've checked on them plenty of times already," Nurse Atropos replied. She tutted and used her pen to point out something on the paper in front of her to the other two nurses. "You're sure decreasing her medication is the way to go?" she asked Nurse Clotho.

"I checked her charts just a short time ago. A low dose would be better, and counselling combined with that should set her on the right path in no time."

Nurse Atropos regarded the youngest nurse sceptically. "A short term stay wasn't on the books for her. What do you think has changed?"

Nurse Clotho smiled, and across the room, Theo decided he had heard enough. He bolted for the door.

Black Springs, Fifth Floor
November 21st
Victor stepped into the elevator as though he were frictionless, his massive arms hanging limply at his sides as he wafted into the metal box like a deflated balloon. He made his way to the back of the box and leaned against its rail, as though the shaft had suddenly become submerged in water and it were the only thing keeping him afloat.

Jaycee stepped in behind him, hitting his shoulder off the doorframe as he did. He wasn't paying attention to his surroundings or the people he passed or the nurses who continued to give him the hairy eyebrow – only to Victor. He stood in the center of the elevator as the doors closed behind him and watched this man – one of the strongest, he thought, that he had ever met – struggle for breath without making so much as a twitch by way of an outward sign.

It seemed to be a contradiction, but it wasn't. Normal men, the men Jaycee had know growing up in Idaho, could have punched the wall or fallen to the floor or wept into the sleeves of their shirts and still have been considered to have 'taken it well'... but for Victor, from whom Jaycee had come to expect nothing short of economy of movement, no motion unneeded or unaccounted for, just the slight motion of his eyes from one side to the other, the twitch of his nostrils, and the way his hand kept moving half-way to his face, getting lost, and then finding a place to rest: just those things were enough to make it clear to Jean-Claude Maximus that Victor was not, by any stretch of the imagination, taking this well.

Victor moved a hand up and slicked back his long blonde hair, his fingers acting like the thick teeth of a comb. His eyes focused on nothing, continuing back to a small spot on the floor between himself and Jaycee that was invisible to anyone else.

His tongue felt like the bed of a desert in his mouth, but after a few moments Jaycee couldn't stand the silence anymore. "It's going to be okay."

"I know," Victor said, without meeting his eye. He remained motionless for a moment, sniffed twice, then straightened his posture. He turned back to Jaycee and nodded once. "I know."

"Should one of us tell his mother?"

"I don't think so. And I'm honestly ready to get out of here. Los Angeles hasn't been particularly kind to me."

Jaycee nodded, then reached over and pressed the

"M" button on the elevator's keypad. The light encircling it glowed a harsh bright red. He cracked his large, swollen knuckles.

Victor stopped and eyed him, looking him up and down for the first time since they'd left Caleb's room. "Are *you* okay?"

His lip twitched. On anyone else's face it might have mirror the nasal spasm that Victor's face had been making, but Jaycee lacked the nostrils that would have made that possible. "Hn? Yeah. Yeah. I'm just... It's a lot."

Victor nodded, then dug his phone out of his pocket and started to type. After a moment's silence he put his phone away again. "Look at it this way: the worst of it is behind us."

Jaycee nodded.

The elevator made a sharp bing.

The mirror-shone metal doors opened.

Theo Flaherty raised his head and saw them, stopping mid-stride as he was about to enter the elevator. "You."

Victor was away from the back of the elevator before the syllable was even complete. He grabbed Theo by the scruff of his shirt and pulled him inside, spinning him as he did and pushing his back against the wall of the lift with gritted teeth.

"Jesus," Jaycee spat, stepping behind Victor and blocking the view from the lobby as the doors closed behind them.

"Months," Victor breathed, his voice barely restrained. His hands released Theo and he pushed back. His hands lowered, neither completely at rest by his sides nor raised to strike, but clenching the air as if hungry for something between them. "Months with no word."

The elevator chimed as though someone on another floor had called it.

"Victor," Jaycee said sternly.

Victor turned and hit the emergency stop button, almost without looking. All of the LEDs on the panel flashed harsh *red*.

"Jesus," Jaycee repeated.

"I'm sorry," Theo said, his eyes oscillating between angry defiance and honest regret. "Things came up that couldn't wait. I didn't have the time or the luxury of waiting for your say-so."

Victor's hands came up, resting against the wall on either side of Theo's head. He took several long, strained breaths through his nostrils before speaking. "We could have used you in Atlanta. People died that might not have died had you been there. Because you were... what? Chasing some girl again like a broken record?" He slammed his fist against the wall, then immediately let the fingers loosen.

In Theo's mind's eye, he could see it all behind Victor and Jaycee, like a billboard that took up the entirety of the far wall of the elevator. Soundless gifs of Quinn and Kat and Gavin were playing. The images started off crisp in clean unfiltered HD, but after a moment it was like some unseen Director of Photography added increasingly dark red filters to the camera lens. The images became more and more overshadowed by the colors until all that existed on the wall behind Victor and Jaycee was red.

He shook his head clear of the image. "It was Leigh, Victor!" he spat finally, physically pushing Victor's hands away from him without success. "Leigh was dying!"

Victor stopped, his lips curling. He stared at Theo for a long time, almost looking past him. The two men locked eyes for a long, tense moment. Behind them, Jaycee paced back and forth, continually checking the flashing lights of the elevator as if expecting them to change color or tempo. Finally, Victor lowered his hands and straightened his shirt with one tug, and took a step back from Theo. "How is she now?"

"She's gone," he said, pushing himself off from the wall and rubbing his shoulder. All at once, it was like saying the words made them true. Even as a great weight was added to his heart, an even greater weight was lifted from his shoulders. He nodded twice. "Leigh's gone."

"I'm sorry," Victor said.

"Yeah, I'm not," Jaycee mumbled from over his shoulder.

"There's someone else though, someone who needs help," Theo said quickly. Then, in a lower voice, "A girl."

"Shocking."

"Jean-Claude," Victor said evenly.

Jaycee's head snapped around. "You *just* said --"

"This place is bad," Theo said finally, touching Victor on the arm as he did. Victor turned and looked at it, but said nothing. "You must have noticed it if you've been here any time at all... or maybe you haven't, but I *grew up here*, Victor."

At that, Victor stiffened. "Does she have a name?"

"Alice," Theo said, and it came out as a sigh of relief. "Alice Loveless."

Victor turned and pressed the emergency stop button

on the elevator, then the button for the fourth floor. The elevator jolted to life and the lights stopped flashing red.

"Yeah, nobody will have any questions about that," Jaycee mumbled under his breath.

Victor straightened his shirt again. "Tell me everything you can."

∞

The three men entered the fourth floor together. The card reader glowed ominously red as they exited the elevator, and leading the way toward it, Theo withdrew the cardkey from his pocket. He tried it twice, only for an angry beep to spring forth from the panel each time. He paled slightly, and Jaycee pushed him out of the way. "Let me."

He popped the panel off the wall with surprising ease, revealing a mess of wire and circuitry. With one hand he pressed down hard on the door handle, and with the other he twisted as many wires together as he could and yanked hard. An electric pop accompanied sparks as he did so, and the handle gave away under his other hand, the door swinging open. Jaycee shot a devilish grin at Victor and Theo. "After you."

The nurses' station was empty as they entered. The desk Clotho, Lachesis, and Atropos had stood around moments before had been vacated. "I thought you said you tore out of here like a bat out of hell," Victor said, eyeing Theo.

"I did, lucky break I g-" Theo started, falling to his knees and clutching his head. "Fuck," he hissed, eyes slammed shut. The burning smell filled his nostrils yet again.

He bit down on a strap, eyes wide and fighting, Doctor Augustus looming over him. Then it was Doctor Brakman. Then it was Doctor Augustus. Their faces melted together.

Theo's eyes shot open, and the room around him swam. Victor reached down and hoisted him up by his armpits, bringing him eyelevel. "What are you seeing?" he asked Theo gruffly.

Head lolling as he fought the pain, Theo replied. "I honestly don't know anymore."

Jaycee rolled his eyes. "C'mon, man, pull it together."

Victor looked at Jaycee and then around the room before looking back at Theo. Each hallway, every door, the windows that would never open, and all the obstacles around them seemed to form an inventory in his mind before he locked eyes with the younger man. "You're getting out of here now, understand? I put you in that elevator, I hand you the keys, and I count on you to be waiting with the El Dorado when Jaycee and I get the girl out of here."

Theo nodded, and Victor let go of him, reaching for his pocket. Theo seemed to float for a moment, body swaying in the air, and then suddenly he began to drop. Victor grabbed him again quickly. "Change of plans. Theo, which way to that damn doctor? Jaycee, you're heading to her and keeping her busy, I'm chucking his butt in the elevator and circling back for the girl."

Theo's face contorted, fighting the pain rolling over him. "She's down the left hall, turn right twice when you get to the end, then through the big doors," he grunted. "She was in her office when I left her, with the hall full of glass doors; you shouldn't miss her."

Jaycee nodded. "Got it."

Looping his arm around Theo to support him, Victor took one last look at Jaycee before heading back out the door. "I trust you, kid."

CHAPTER 27

November 21st

Leigh's stomach churned as the car pulled in through the compound gates. They paused briefly, and through the divider Leigh could hear the muffled sounds of their driver speaking to the guard, though she couldn't make out what was said. She fought the urge to clench her hands tightly, knowing her white knuckles would surely reveal her nerves to Hale if she did.

The divider slid open without warning, light streaming into the darkened car, and Hale leaned forward to accept an envelope from the driver. Leigh was almost blinded by the drastic difference. Hale nodded in thanks though, shutting the divider just as abruptly as it had been opened and returned to his seat to rifle through the contents of the envelope. The car began to pull forward again, and he settled in for the short remainder of their journey.

Happy to find everything in order, he handed the envelope to Leigh without removing anything. She took it hesitantly, eyeing him quizzically as she did so. "Your credentials for the base," he explained, smiling cordially.

She nodded in understanding, peering into the envelope briefly herself before deciding to simply dump the contents in her lap. An electronic ID card on a retractable cord spilt out, though where they had gotten her picture for it she had no idea, and so did several sheets of paper and a pen. She looked back up at Hale for an explanation.

"Your waivers and contracts are all there. You can read over them and sign now if you like, or you can take some time to look at them later this evening. It's just to cover our obligations and yours, as well as all the nasty stuff like next-of-kin should anything happen to you while you're on assignment," he said.

She looked down at the sheets, scanning them. "No next-of-kin to worry about," she replied. "I'm a no-strings-attached kind of girl."

Hale raised an eyebrow, smiling a little. "And yet you're anything but, the kind of woman who is exactly as she seems. I'm glad we'll be working together, Ms. Blackheart."

She looked up at him, taking a moment to scan his face before she replied. "Me too, Director."

Hale smiled as she bowed her head and uncapped the pen, scanning each sheet for lines that required her signature. She flipped through them all when she was finished, double-checking her work, then slipped the sheets back into the envelope and handed it back to Hale. "That should all be in order now," she said smiling.

"Perfect," Hale replied, tucking the envelope into his suitcase. "We'll head to the Mess Hall first for some lunch, and then I'll show you around personally. Once you get settled in, I'm sure it'll be a big weight off your shoulders."

"Exactly," Leigh said, relaxing a little more. "It'll be nice to have the run of the place and have some freedom again."

Hale chuckled. "I'm sure it will. The manhunt has been officially called off for you now too, so you can look forward to walking around without looking over your shoulder as much."

"I appreciate that immensely. I could have dealt with it well enough, but it's good to have the burden off my back."

"What are friends for if not to make life a little easier?" Hale chuckled.

Leigh could feel the car slow to a stop. She heard the driver open and close his door before opening hers, standing square as she nimbly exited the vehicle. Straightening, she smoothed out her pants and clipped her new ID card to her waistband. When she looked up, she found herself in the middle of slick looking metal buildings, all low and sprawling. In her head, she had imagined it would be large, but not quite this large.

"Welcome to Circe," Hale said, getting out of the car and standing behind her. "Or I suppose I should say, welcome home."

Leigh tried to smile but managed only a weak one. She would have to get used to thinking of this as "home."

CHAPTER 28

Black Springs, Fourth Floor
November 21st
Victor loped down the long sterile hallway, looking entirely out of place: his black shirt and dark jeans sticking out against the clean white of the hospital like a contrast photo. He turned around, aware of the people looking at him, his gaze shifting from one to the other until finally landing on Nurse Susan, sitting behind the desk at the Nurse's Station, eyeing him quizzically.

Forcing composure upon himself, he walked over to her and smiled. "Hey."

"Hey," she said, her voice low.

Victor nodded. "I understand." He paused for effect, counting the seconds in his mind until he looked up and met her eye again, his face full of a manufactured smile. "I'm not sure if you can help, but I could really use a wheelchair for my niece."

Susan smiled.

Black Springs, Fourth Floor
November 21st

Jaycee stalked down the glowing hall, his contorted face set in a grimace. The place was too froufrou for his liking, the lemony scent hanging in the air irritating his nose. It reminded him of the old Southern women he had grown up knowing, the ones who masked their vile personalities behind a bottle of perfume and the phrase "bless your heart."

He peered in each room as he walked by, trying to figure out if Doctor Augustus was behind the frosted glass or not. The majority of rooms he walked by seemed to be empty laboratories or treatment rooms, though for what sort of treatment he couldn't be sure. From what he could make out, there were far too many sharp objects around for a psych ward.

A sound caused Jaycee's head to shoot up, his eyes drawn to the noise. Just a few doors down from him, a tall woman exited a door and stopped dead in her tracks, looking him up and down. She paused for a moment, waiting to see if he would make the next move.

"Hey there," he started.

The woman straightened out, her surprise thawing. "Can I help you?" she asked.

Jaycee chuckled. "Yeah, actually, looking for a Doctor Augustus. I was told I could come down this way for a little help with all of this," he said, motioning in a circle around his face.

The woman's eyes narrowed. "I don't do plastic surgery; you were given the wrong name," she said.

"You misunderstand," Jaycee chuckled again. "I don't do plastic surgery either. I just heard you were good with my particular set of problems."

Doctor Augustus relaxed a little, but still seemed to evaluate him. "Come in then," she said, reopening the door to her office.

Jaycee followed her in, taking a seat across from her desk. Neither took their eyes off the other as they sat down, though Doctor Augustus retrieved a fresh file folder and pen from her desk drawer. She left the drawer open, but placed the file on her desk, uncapping the pen before she spoke.

"Tell me about yourself," she commanded.

"Well, I've been this way for as long as I can remember," Jaycee started flippantly. "It's great to be 'unique' and all," he said, adding air quotes. "But it kinda gets on my nerves when my girlfriend's family goes all murdery on me because I look like some alien-lovechild-burn victim, even if I do get a little extra strength out of the weird gene mix. Might be nice not to be shot at next time I try heading home for a bit."

Doctor Augustus' eyes narrowed. "You're awfully jovial for someone who claims he's almost been killed for the way he looks."

Jaycee smiled, revealing his pointed grin. "Yeah, well, you're awfully suspicious for someone who's supposed to help people."

The words hung in the air for a moment, Doctor Augustus' face souring as she regarded him. "I take it you're one of the friends Theo was talking about then?" she asked.

Jaycee threw his hands up mockingly. "You caught me, I jacked up my face just to come up here and torment you after a bad patient meeting."

Doctor Augustus straight up glowered. "Try a plastic surgeon, this town has tons of them," she spat.

"Nah," Jaycee replied. "I think I'll keep trying my luck with you," he said, leaning forward in his chair to bridge the gap between them.

As he did so, Doctor Augustus reached into her desk drawer, pulling out a small revolver and pointing it at him. "Don't toy with me," she hissed.

This time, Jaycee's hands shot up without even a hint of mockery. "Hey now, I just opened up and told you I have a thing about guns pointing my way. Let's just calm down here, no need to get nasty."

Doctor Augustus clicked the safety off. "Not for one second am I going to let you come in here and intimidate me over my life's work, understand?" she hissed.

"Completely understood, ma'am. My apologies," Jaycee said slowly, staring down the barrel of the gun.

Doctor Augustus stood up, gun still trained on him. "You think anyone will be able to do anything if you don't come out of here? I've got the senator on speed dial. Six different prosecutors owe me a favour. No one will be able to do shit for some jacked up looking punk. No one will be able to find you when I'm through with you," she snapped.

The colour drained from Jaycee's face. "Alternatively," he proposed. "You could just let me walk out of here and we can call it a day? No need for violence, and we go our separate ways all hunky dory."

Chuckling, Doctor Augustus shook her head. "Tell me, have you been bullshitting me since you got here, or is there some shred of truth to your story, Mr. Super-strength?"

Jaycee looked at her like she had ten heads. "Do I look like someone who gets away with lying often?" he asked, half joking.

A spark flashed in Doctor Augustus' eyes. "I'll enjoy studying you then," she said, hands moving as she fired at him.

Jaycee sprang out of the way as she did so, feeling the heat of the bullet against his arm as he did so. The glass behind him shattered, crashing to the ground angrily. The room reeked of gunpowder.

"Christ, woman!" he yelled. "Glass houses!"

Doctor Augustus strode around the desk as he scrambled backwards, leering over him. She raised the weapon, preparing to shoot again without saying a word. This time, Jaycee didn't give her the chance to shoot.

He lunged, hitting her with his shoulder in her midsection. He heard the gun go off again, and it sounded this time as if it had hit off metal. They fell to the ground struggling, Doctor Augustus bringing the gun up to hit Jaycee in the temple. The assault sent spots dancing in front of his eyes, but he kept fighting, pinning her legs down with his own. "I don't want to hurt you," he pleaded, grunting as she kneed him in the stomach.

She raised her arm with the gun to hit him again, but this time he rolled off her to avoid the smack. She took advantage of this blunder to try and pin him then, lunging at him with gun still in hand. Jaycee looked up at her wide-eyed as his head cracked solidly against the floor, shooting pain through his scalp. Clumsily, he attempted to catch her wrist as she brought the gun close to him, but both missed as they moved. The pain throbbing through his skull screamed concussion, and the sickening realization filled the pit of his stomach that he would be nursing it tenderly later, if he were alive to tell the tale.

His hand shot out for hers again in a mad struggle for the gun as she knelt above him and aimed, and the only thing he could think to do was shove her hands away from him as he attempted to scramble out from under her. The pit of his stomach twanged hard as he heard the gun go off for the third time, this time hot blood spraying across his face. He sat frozen for a moment unsure if it was he who had been shot, or if it was she.

With mixed relief and horror, he realized it had been Doctor Augustus when his eyes found her face. The bullet had skimmed over the bottom of her jaw and torn into her cheekbone and shattered her eye socket, tearing her skin as it went. With horrible surety, he recognized the heated flesh around the entrance of the wound, the tell tale sign the muzzle of the gun had been close enough to burn her at the time it was fired. Through the throbbing pain in his head only one phrase emerged:

"I've killed her," he whispered. As he spoke the words, he clapped a hand over his mouth, as if wishing the phrase had never danced across his tongue. The blood on his cheeks smeared as he did so, and for a moment he sat paralyzed.

Then he ran.

CHAPTER 29

Black Springs, Fourth Floor

November 21st

"Well, it seems like all the charts check out. There's a slight issue with your pancreas and maybe something going on with your prostate, but other than that you should be good to go," Victor said, pushing the wheelchair into the room until it bumped up against the bed and jostled it.

Alice's head turned toward him sharply, though she strained to move, her knees and arms clearly fighting against restraints underneath the bedcovers. "Who are you?" she whispered, panic edging her voice.

Victor left the wheelchair and craned his head around the divider in the room. "And the things with the prostate, they can get out of control fast. You don't want that thing to just start eating your food on you, because then there won't be enough left for... the stomach. The prostate is basically just a giant natural... tape worm." He opened the door to Alice's bathroom, poked his head inside, and then ducked back out. "You're alone, good. I'm not good at medical jargon."

She grimaced at him, panic still clear on her face.

"My name is Victor, I'm a friend of Theo's," he said conspiratorially, and her eyes lit up. "We're getting you out of here."

"Get these bands off quickly, please," she pleaded. "They're cutting in so tight."

"Obliged," Victor said, pulling back the sheets and unbuckling the wrist closest to him. "No restraints like this where we're going." He paused for a moment then. "Unless you need them, that is. You're not going to get all violent on me, are you?" he joked

She shook her head fearfully as he moved to the next wrist. "Where's Theo?"

"Waiting outside."

Victor finished with her wrists and then moved to one of her ankles while she sat up and attacked the other. Her dressing gown was thin, almost floating around her as she moved. When they were finished, she sprung from the bed, the bruises on her wrists and ankles an angry purple against her skin.

"Hop in the chair," Victor instructed.

She gave him an odd look, one eyebrow raised.

"We're going to try and fly under the radar here. This needs to look normal."

She complied, and his eyes darted around the room for a pair of slippers, which he grabbed from beside her bed. He knelt down to tuck them on her feet, and then folded the comforter from her bed across her lap quickly, sheltering her legs.

"Ready?" he asked.

She nodded.

He turned her around and pushed her out the door into the hallway. The bright white of the hall assaulted them again; so different from the dim, muted lighting she kept in her room. She squinted and raised her hand against it, inadvertently showing him the series of tiny red dots from multiple injections and IVs. He grimaced, and they made their way down the hallway toward the elevator.

There was an old woman with matted gray hair sitting on a stool across from the nurses' station. She was missing one eye, the remnants of it milky and green, and the good eye, almond-shaped and brown, watched them go. She worked her jaw as if she were chewing on something, but was not. Across from her, Susan sat and watched as they moved, slowly but deliberately, down the hall. She bit her lip, her eyes going from Victor to Alice and then back again, as if unsure of what to do.

"Easy does it," he said almost inaudibly, so that even Alice could barely hear him. He nodded to Susan, then turned back toward the elevator door.

"Is this the whole plan?" she asked, faking a smile and a relaxed tone of voice.

"Your Doctor is being distracted."

"I assumed. But still, walking out was the whole plan?"

"Essentially."

"It's a good plan."

Susan finally reached down to something out of view behind the desk, and returned with a phone. She pressed a single button on it and, after a moment, began to speak.

Her eyes never left Victor. "Fuck," he said, picking up his gait slightly. "We're made."

An orderly came out of one of the rooms smiling and laughing to someone else inside, a well-mannered patient presumably. He was tall with a wide chest that was broadest across the shoulders, the very epitome of the term barrel-chested. His hair was slicked back in a widow's peak and there was a noticeable gap between all the teeth in his top row when he laughed, indicating that one had been removed at some point in the past and all the others had shifted to be evenly spaced.

The man's smile vanished when he turned and saw Alice, though his gaze immediately went to Victor and remained there. His hand came up to just under his breastbone and remained there, perched like a bird in mid-step and he finished exiting the room and shut the room behind him.

"Seal," Victor said under his breath. The word came out with the inflection of a curse.

"What?" Alice asked, resisting the urge to turn around and face him.

In the reflection of the metal scratch-guard that lined the walls where they met the chairs, he could see that the man was following them... not directly behind them, in fact he was allowing them to gain minute distance between the two, but he remained directly behind Victor and out of his normal peripheral vision.

Victor's upper lip stiffened. "How many years have you been here?"

"Four."

"How many people have you heard of escaping?"

"Escaping?"

"Leaving, without you knowing they were leaving beforehand and saying goodbye and that."

"From Black Springs? No one I know has really tried, except for me, and I haven't managed since they moved me to this ward. Downstairs, it's easier. Up here the door scanners are too much for me to beat."

He turned. They were thirty feet from the elevator, and from the hallway to its right she saw another orderly appear, a large black man with a clip-board that looked like a child's toy compared to the size of him. He made small marks on it as he stood, framed in a window that led from the hall to the nurse's station. He wrote aimlessly, as though he were just ticking off the seconds by checking the same box over and over again.

"Great," Victor nodded. "I like being first. There's something cathartic about it."

This time she did turn around, no longer worried about how it looked. "What?"

"You know, like the uncharted parts of a map or your first time with someone new," he reasoned, bobbing his head from side to side. "Here be dragons."

"Who have you been with?" she asked jokingly, though without managing to keep her nerves from creeping through.

He smiled. It did not last long.

He turned to open the door to the elevator with his back. Jaycee's little smash and spark trick had negated the need for a cardkey nicely, but that only served to further peak the interest of the orderlies. Backing Alice's wheelchair into the barrier room, he held his breath as the men hastened their pace to follow him through the door. He pressed the button alongside the elevator and waiting, sucking in air so that his cheeks puffed out and then letting it out. Alice tapped her hand against her knee. He took three of these deep breaths before glancing out through the glass in the door to look at the black orderly nearing the door a few feet away from him.

Victor braced the door with his arm and turned his cheek to look down the hallway in time to see a third orderly (or possibly a male nurse, he had a hard time telling the difference) come out of an adjacent room. This new man was thin and short and shut the door he was coming from quietly before locking eyes with the other two orderlies and making his way for the door.

The elevator chimed, the light above it turning on.

"People I worked with, mostly," Victor said softly.

"Hmm?"

"You asked who I've been with."

"I was joking."

"I know." He nodded.

The elevator doors opened and he stepped inside, swivelling the chair with a two-point turn so that they faced back out into the hall. The black man and the short man were not visible now, but the man with the widow's peak was within view of the window: his eyes, the peak of his hair, and his pelvis all seemed to be pointing directly at them.

Alice reached forward and pressed the "M" button, which responded by glowing harsh red at her just as it had for Jaycee. She let her finger slide down imperceptivity and also pressed the button to make the doors close, then sat back in her chair and tried to look anywhere but at the man with the widow's peak, but there simply wasn't anything else in the plain white atmosphere to see.

He stared at her, and the doors weren't closing.

"They should close right away when you press the button," she huffed.

"Read somewhere the button doesn't even do anything. That all it does is make the LED light up, but it's supposed to give people a sense of agency."

"Where'd you read that?"

Victor didn't answer, his eyes locked forward on the man with the widow's peak, as if daring him to make a move.

Finally, the doors began to close.

Alice let out a sigh of relief.

"Okay when we get downstairs--"

The elevator doors stopped suddenly, less than three inches from meeting. Four black fingers with clear, well-manicured nails had appeared just below the center of the left door, as if from nowhere, and Alice jumped in her seat. The scene hung in the air as though they had come unstuck from time for a moment, the tension making everything silent. She couldn't remember when the last time she had heard Black Springs sound so silent, without the ambient whirr of ventilation and the stir of machinery in her ears.

The gears of the elevator switched their tracks and reversed, and the doors opened again. From off to one side the black orderly stepped in and across the two of them, wedging himself in between the wall and Victor's right shoulder. The man with the widow's peak and the space between his teeth was there now too. He smiled and Victor was finally able to place what the man reminded him of: he looked like Robert De Niro did in *Cape Fear*. The association did little to soothe his nerves. He stepped in and took his place to Victor's left, so that he and Alice were now sandwiched between the two.

The elevator doors closed.

The black orderly stepped forward and pressed the button for the second floor.

Victor gripped the rubber handles of Alice's wheelchair so tightly that they emitted a high-pitched squeak as the plastic in them bent under his force, the sound only heard by he and Alice. Moving his tongue around his dry mouth, he extended one finger and tapped her on the shoulder once, then pointed forward.

Alice nodded, almost imperceptivity.

Victor turned to the black man and nodded politely, then to the man with the widow's peak and did the same.

The elevator chimed to let them know they were on the second floor, and the doors opened again. Two more men in white coats, male nurses or orderlies, stepped with storm trooper-like unison into the elevator. They were rectangular and lean. One had tanned orange skin and gray hair, even though he couldn't have been more than thirty, and the other had one of those long faces with bulging jowls that after a few drinks, Victor might have privately joked made him look like a pelican.

Victor smiled and nodded to them both wordlessly as they shuffled to the left and right, respectfully taking their position next to each of the orderlies that had been there before. Victor cleared his throat loudly as the doors to the elevator closed. There was less than a foot of free space where nobody was sitting, just in front of Alice's wheelchair.

"A friend of mine was in the audience during the taping of that episode of Jeopardy, the one where Andy Richter schooled Wolf Blitzer," Victor said finally, making eye contact with Alice via the elevator door's reflection. All four of the orderlies' heads twitched in his direction, but otherwise they did not respond. After a pregnant pause, Victor continued. "Apparently he got drunk on some wine he'd smuggled in between tapings and started saying all these curses and slurs and things that... well, just didn't make any sense. Then he started going on about the Cree and everyone thought he was making some point about the plight of the Native Americans, but it turned out he was talking about the aliens from some comic book, the Kree. Went on like that forever, and it wasn't until he started talking about the Shi'ar and the Skrulls that somebody clued in to what was going on. Alex Trebek had to come over and tell him to shut up and everything."

The orderly with the widow's peak squinted, licked his lips, then turned to face Victor. He stood silently for a moment, then said: "Which one? Andy Richter or Wolf Blitzer?"

Victor turned his head toward him and cocked an eyebrow. "My friend. Why would Andy Richter or Wolf Blitzer act like that?"

Alice dove forward onto the floor in front of her wheelchair as Victor shoved the chair to one side, digging the hard plastic into the crotch of the man with the widow's peak while slamming the metal cage around the wheels into the greying orderly next to him. They both let out a rush of air as the orderly with the pelican jaws pressed the emergency stop button and the elevator ground to a halt, the shift in gravity shaking them all, and the black man gripped Victor around both shoulders with his plump fingers. He pulled hard on Victor's flesh, who felt something small but important strain itself against the man's grasp. He was raised off his feet and immediately started kicking, hitting the chair twice and driving it further into the graying man's midsection and then connecting his heel to Widow's Peak three times, one to the chest and twice to the face. On the third blow, when he bent his knee there was blood on his boot.

The black man wrapped his arm around Victor's throat and started to press, bracing him against his body so that he couldn't butt his head back.

The Pelican-Man removed his hand from his coat pocket, revealing a small cylindrical object. It might have been mistaken for a pager or an electric shaver had there not been blue arcing sparks erupting from the tip. The man jutted it forward towards Victor.

"No!" Alice screamed from her vantage point on the floor, grabbing the man's heal with both hands and pulling. He jolted to the right and Victor, lips already a deep purple, knocked his elbow into the elbow of the man holding him. His arm bounced up and into the path of the Taser. The man screamed, the fillings in his teeth arcing electricity and his muscles tightened, pulling Victor's neck even closer to him before relaxing altogether.

Victor took a deep breath and slid his head out from

the meat of the man's arm, then brought his foot up into the midsection of the Pelican's abdomen with the same motion. His foot came down in the space between Alice's arm and torso as she tried to get up, and he grabbed the graying man's head by both ears and brought it down onto his knee before releasing it again.

Alice looked up in horror, scrambling to her feet now to get away from the blood that the man with the widow's peak had begun to cough. The black man was slumped in a heap in the corner and the Pelican-Man was gasping for air. The Taser lay on the floor beside her. She grabbed it and pressed it into the man's thigh, who jolted wordlessly then fell to the floor as well. Scrambling to her feet, Victor turned off the elevator's emergency stop. The cables and gears lurched back to life.

The man with the widow's peak smiled. The gap between his teeth was even wider now, as he was missing three. "You're never going to be able to stop running."

"So nothing's changed then," Victor growled, bringing his fist down against the base of the man's neck and knocking him out.

Alice snapped to her feet next to him, turning from one assailant to the other. Her breath came in short huffs that she tried desperately to make longer but her lungs refused her. "Walk out, huh? Do all your plans work out this well?"

"No," he frowned, taking the Taser from her and pocketing it. "Sometimes things really go south."

The elevator doors chimed and opened to the main lobby and they stepped out just in time to see Jaycee exit the stairwell on the other side. "Jay!" Victor yelled, getting his attention.

Alice jolted at the look of Jaycee briefly, but shrugged it off as she heard a groan from the elevator behind them.

Jaycee ran over to them, out of breath. "This place, Victor. This place is so fucked up."

"Gathered that," Victor nodded.

"This her?"

He nodded.

"Where's Theo?"

The glass doors of Black Springs burst in as the receptionist, who was in the process of walking over to Victor and Jaycee, screamed. Alarms started blaring as the El Dorado burst into the lobby, its engine revving and screaming and the car spun on its wheels and came to a stop alongside the trio. Theo shoved his head out the window: "Get in!"

They got in and Theo slammed the car into gear, leaving through another hole in the glass instead of the ones they came in through and ignoring the chime of the seatbelt signal.

"Glad to see you're feeling better, but was that really necessary?" Victor growled, brushing safety glass out of Alice's hair.

"Fuck no," Theo smirked. "That was cathartic."

CHAPTER 30

November 21st

Theo opened the door to his apartment and left the keys in the knob, dangling against the turn wooden frame. The four of them – he, Victor, Jaycee, and Alice – were in before they finished jangling. He ran to the TV stand and opened it, revealing several boxes whose exteriors were lined with red felt. He scooped them up haphazardly, reached behind them, and took out a hockey bag. "We can't stay here," he said without looking up from what he was doing.

"I agree," said Victor, even as he took Theo's coats off the rack and laid them on the kitchen table. "And I don't mean this apartment. I don't think Los Angeles is going to be safe for us for a little while."

"Think they'll call the police?" Jaycee asked, as he watched the two men work.

"I think that's the least of our worries," Victor mumbled under his breath. He started throwing the jackets on top of the same hockey bag that Theo was filling, making no attempt to organize anything. He turned to Jaycee: "Go in the bedroom and--"

He stopped when he looked at the younger man, who had backed up so that his exposed shoulder blade touched the cool wall of Theo's apartment. Victor's eyes enlarged slightly and he rose to stand ramrod straight, dropping the jackets to the floor.

"What?" Jaycee asked, his fingers laced together and feeling the knuckles of the hand opposite.

Victor stepped forward and grabbed him by the crook of his arm, forcing him into the bedroom and slamming the door behind them.

Theo and Alice looked up.

"What was that about?" she asked.

"Not a nap," he sighed.

Victor stopped and stepped back from Jaycee, looking him up and down several times. His eyes lingered on the drops of blood, though they also searched in vain for the source. Finally, Victor reached up and forced Jaycee's head to the side, exposing the beginnings of bruising along the man's temple.

"Hey!" Jaycee winced.

He dropped his hand, satisfied and disgusted at the same time. "What happened with the Doctor?"

Jaycee winced, then sat on the bed and buried his head in his three-fingered hands.

"What. Happened," he said again, with force behind each syllable.

"I mean, I started like you said, she was... I didn't have a choice," Jaycee started, his voice wet as he spoke into his hands. "It's not like Sherriff Lane from back home or anybody back there or anything we dealt with. I don't know what else I could have done."

Victor nodded, even though Jaycee couldn't see it.

Jaycee sniffed back and pulled away from his hands, which were shaking. When he looked back at Victor, his eyes were red and moist. "I was just going to talk to her... it wasn't meant to be like that. She was too suspicious, too quick... I really did try, I just couldn't..." He cut himself off, unable to finish the sentence.

Victor nodded, kneeling so that he was in Jaycee's line of sight. "Did you kill her?"

Jaycee started to shake his head, then stopped himself and nodded. "It's a hospital. It's where you're supposed to be able to bring your kids to get better and she's using it like some kind of genetic buffet for her research. She would have hurt hundreds, maybe thousands. Who knows what she was planning on using the research for."

Victor nodded. "You can't see into the future though, to know how things might have turned out."

"Something in me just... panicked. I've never felt that way before. It was like there were flies in my head behind my eyes," he brought his fingers up to his bald head and pressed them in. "Just buzzing around and making it hard to think and making it hard to see, but I could see what she was doing and what she was going to do. I can't imagine what she'd have done if she realized about Caleb--" he looked up into Victor's face, and his own went pale. Instead of the sympathy he had been expecting, he saw reserved resignation, sadness... and anger.

"We can't kill," he said, simply and firmly. "It goes against... everything. It... it just goes against it."

Jaycee nodded. "I know, I'm sorry. I just didn't see

another way."

"I can't have murderers on the team or in my presence."

"You won't. I'm sorry. I just couldn't do anything. I thought she was going to kill me. I really did; I thought she was going to kill me."

Victor stood slowly, then backed away from Jaycee until his back was against the wall.

Jaycee looked up at him again and tilted his head to one side. "Wait, what are you saying?"

Victor did not move for several tense moments, but then motioned toward the door.

Jaycee turned and looked at it, as if expecting Theo to come in or for it to do something, anything really, then turned back to Victor. "I get that I fucked up here, but you can't have violence without accidents happening --"

"Jean-Claude."

"Things are going to happen. Theo could have hit someone when he came in through the glass at Black Springs or one of the guys from the elevator could have choked and died, you don't know. You can't always--"

"Jean-Claude."

"-know what's going to happen," Jaycee's voice raised now, his eyes lowering and no longer moist. "You always think you know, but you don't. You can't see the future; you don't know where all this is heading! The world is in trouble, that's what you said, but it's in trouble because of people like--"

"*Maximus*," Victor barked.

He stopped talking.

After a long moment of the two men looking at each

other, Victor turned and nodded toward the door again. When he spoke again, his voice was low, almost a deep whisper: "You're exiled."

Jaycee got up without looking at him, left the room, walked past Theo and Alice, and out of the apartment. A moment later, Victor came out of the room as well, fishing his phone out of his pocket.

"What the hell was that about?" Theo asked, zipping up his hockey bag and putting it over his shoulder.

Victor looked down at the screen. The message he had been typing in the elevator earlier was still pending: 'There's something wrong with JC.' He paused and regarded it for some time, then deleted each character and typed, 'Maximus is gone' before hitting send.

CHAPTER 31

November 22nd

Theo sat in the passenger seat of the El Dorado experiencing an eerie feeling of déjà vu. Victor stared straight ahead in silence, the Arizona interstate calling him home. In the back, Alice slept spread across the seat wearing a pale blue dress Leigh had left hanging in the closet. She had a plush cream throw thrown over her covering her arms and shoulders, and the black boots on her feet came up just high enough to cover her bruises. For the first time, she almost looked like a normal girl to Theo.

Looking at Victor, Theo cleared his throat.

"Unless that's an apology brewing in your throat for slamming my car through glass, you're better off with silence," Victor grumbled.

Theo cocked his head slowly and pursed his lips. "Sorry for ramming your car through glass," he said slowly.

Victor glanced at him out of the corner of his eye. "It doesn't happen again, hear me? No matter how good it feels."

Theo grinned a little, the tension easing slightly. "I

promise."

Victor didn't return the grin though, instead opting to glue his eyes to the road. His face could have been chiselled from stone, his brow stern and his profile unmoving. Theo felt as if the air inside the car would suffocate them in the silence. The grin slid from his face.

"I still love her, you know," he whispered. "I just couldn't love her the right way, I guess. I would have died for her though, if she asked me."

Victor's shoulders softened a little, and he sighed. "You've got to stop bending over backwards for every broken girl you come across," he said finally.

Theo's mouth tightened sadly. "I would have loved her even if she wasn't sick. This is a curse, you know, not a gift. I knew her almost as soon as I met her. You see everyone's life, their good and their bad all laid out like that, it's easy to love them."

Victor glanced at him, face still stern, but softening. "All the more reason not to bend over backwards. Leigh was never some helpless damsel, and you knew that. Same goes for Abby, really. They've always been capable of helping themselves." Victor paused, Theo staring at him pointedly, and then he glanced back at Alice. "Except for her, of course. That was actually kind of handy on your part. To be fair, you've needed help getting out of there multiple times too now, so still try and lose the hero complex."

"Point taken," Theo said, bowing his head in defeat.

Victor seemed to want to fill the silence now that they had started talking, something that Theo could never remember him doing, and now in the confined space of the old El Dorado, the mood seemed to change. "You're young, there's still plenty of time for your whole world to be turned upside down. Right now it feels like she's the one to change your life, but there are bigger things out there, I promise you. If I had known what was in front of me when I was your age, well… I wouldn't have believed it for a moment." Victor paused his story for a moment. "Let me tell you about a good friend of mine."

EPILOGUE

Los Angeles, California

November 25th

Jean-Claude Maximus sat at the bar nursing his third Snake Bite in thirty minutes. It was a drink that Chad Matthews had taught him, composed of tequila and Jack Daniels and cola in equal parts. If it was mixed right – and if the tequila was of a good enough quality – it was supposed to taste like caramel. This drink was not mixed right, and tasted like paint thinner, which did nothing to stop him from drinking more. He finished his third and motioned for another.

"I'll pay for that one," said a large man who came up from behind him and sat on the seat two stools down from him. He was so large that even sitting that far away, he was still sitting next to the man. His skin was ashen and gray and looked like shadow in the dim light of the bar, the muscles of his bare arm pulsing with blood even when he wasn't moving.

"That's okay," Jaycee said, waving the thought away politely. "You don't need to do me any favours." The bartender put his fourth drink in front of him and he grabbed at it as though he thought it were going to get away, then turned and raised it to the man next to him, seeing him for the first time. He was bald and there were raised indentations above his eyes like piercings under the skin that went up his skull until they were out of view. He paused for a moment when he saw that, then laughed at himself. "What would you like to drink to?"

Jona smiled as his own drink was placed in front of him. "How about: to being different?"

Jaycee smiled and nodded, and their glasses touched.

ENGEN TIMELINE

With over twenty novels spread over three different series by many different authors, the Engen Universe of titles is growing every day and into genres we couldn't have imagined! From the original ten book *Black Womb* thriller series, its crime novel sequel series *Xander Drew*, our flagship adventure title *Infinity*, or single-novels like *Jacobi Street* or *light|dark*, there's something in the Engen Universe for everyone with more books by more authors on the way soon!

...But how do the events relate to one another, chrono-logically? While some astute readers have guessed at the potential timeline (some accurately, some not), we're going to finally set the question of the Engen Timeline to rest.

Turn the page for an up-to-date guide of the ever-widening world of Engen, featuring the works of Ellen Curtis, Andrea Hackett, Ali House, Sarah Thompson, Jay Paulin, and Matthew LeDrew!

In the 10 Years Prior Black September

"Reptilia" by Matthew LeDrew published in *light l dark*.
Danger descends on a small secluded town in the form of a deadly virus with fantastic and terrible side-effects. Can a small group of doctors escape alive?

Compendium by Ellen Curtis
Three short stories forming the basis for the Engen Universe's ties to suspense, genetic engeneering, and the supernatural. Features the stories "The Tourniquet Revival," "Falling into Fire" and "At Midnight, the Dawn."

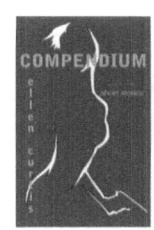

"The Theogony" by Matthew LeDrew published in *light l dark*.
A tale of young Theo Flaherty of the *Infinity* series and his time admitted against his will to the Black Springs hospital, where he learns to paint, and seeks out his father.

Black September

"Revving Engen" by Matthew LeDrew published in *light l dark*.
A direct lead-in to both *Infinity* and *Black Womb*, Tasha travels to Coral Beach, Maine on a hot tip about a recently discovered young man with incredible abilities.

Infinity by Ellen Curtis & Matthew LeDrew
Faced with a destiny he's uncertain of, the enigmatic Victor must bring together four unique people with very special abilities… or face the tasks ahead alone. Guaranteed to excite!

Black Womb by Matthew LeDrew
Fifteen years ago, something happened in Coral Beach, Maine that resulted in the present death of a seventeen-year-old boy. Now four high-school students must try to solve the mystery... before the killer picks them off.

Jacobi Street by Matthew LeDrew
When a mysterious painting shows up at an art gallery he works at, Bob must work with Eddie and Sloan to track down its sinister origins and convince the people living on Jacobi Street of them, before its too late!

Transformations in Pain by Matthew LeDrew
When two girls are assaulted and one is hospitalized, the residents of Coral Beach must put their shared tragedies behind them and stop the man responsible, as well as unlock the secrets behind the true nature of the Womb...

Year One: October

Smoke and Mirrors by Matthew LeDrew
The approaching trial of Genblade brings closure to the people of Coral Beach, until people start showing up dead in the same manner they did when he was at large.

"Scarlett" by Andrea Hackett
published in *light I dark*.
Introducing Scarlett, the slightly damaged hunter on a mission to save others from the monsters from her past.

"The Inevitable" by Ali House
published in *The Lightbulb Forest*
A young woman must contend with the
emergence of a frightening new power alongside
the emotional high of a first date.

The Tourniquet Reprisal by Curtis & LeDrew
A man lives in Atlanta, Georgia that people
don't talk about, but everyone knows he's there.
He arrived a year ago and turned a gaggle
of uneducated youth into something new,
something to fear.

Roulette by Matthew LeDrew
As the teen suicide rate in Coral Beach starts to
climb astronomically fast, Xander travels to Los
Angeles to fight his most terrifying adversary
yet… and learns that the only thing worse than
looking for release… is finding it.

Year One: November

Exodus of Angels by Curtis & LeDrew
Victor's enigmatic past is illuminated when
Jaycee accompanies him to visit a new friend
in the paliative care ward of the Black Springs
hospital, where Theo also happens to be
searching for a cure for Leigh.

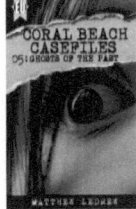

Ghosts of the Past by Matthew LeDrew
Coral Beach faces its most awesome threat when
one of Engen's past mistakes is unleashed upon
the unsuspecting populous. Friends and enemies
unite to fight a common enemy… but will even
that be enough?

Touch Your Nose by Matthew LeDrew
Simon Monk must infiltrate the San Fransico
branch of Shane Industries, a massive company
with deep ties to the Engen Universe. Where do
his true loyalties lie? And can he get out without
causing harm?

Ignorance is Bliss by Matthew LeDrew
After being set through the ringer one too many
times, Xander decides that his life with Julie
needs a little more attention… which is bad news
because a new villain has come to town with his
sights set on Adam Genblade.

"Gristle While You Work" by Jay Paulin
published in *light | dark*.
A short story centering around the rise of a new,
and possibly cannibalistic, serial killer in the
Engen Universe.

Becoming by Matthew LeDrew
For months Xander Drew has been doing his
level best to keep the streets of Coral Beach clean,
which means it's time for the forces of darkness to
strike back… all at once.

Inner Child by Matthew LeDrew
Julie is hospitalized with life-threatening wounds
to both body and soul. But the real threat comes
from the hospital walls themselves, as a demonic
presence makes itself known to Xander and his
friends.

End of Year One

Gang War by Matthew LeDrew
The Tees, a homicidal gang of evil men, has finally been taken down by Xander Drew. But his victory is short lived, as retired Tees are mysteriously killed. With a town of suspects, anyone can be the culprit… including one of their own.

Chains by Matthew LeDrew
Sociopath Derek Smith has been freed from prison and is praying on the weak; and none are weaker than August Styles: a pregnant girl with Down Syndrome who has run away from home.

"Omega" by Ellen Curtis
published in *light | dark*.
A sinister division of Engen begins a series of experiments on pregnant women in a fashion eerily similar to those that created the original Black Womb project.

The Long Road by Matthew LeDrew
Xander meets the American people — and realizes that the world is harsh and wicked, but can also be soft and gentle, even loving. Xander Drew comes of age on the road, and sets his new direction.

Year Two

Cinders by Matthew LeDrew
Detective Horton enters a violent and dangerous world he didn't know existed beneath the veneer of order and structure that he has based his entire deductive method around.

Sinister Intent by Matthew LeDrew
One of the killers Detective Horton could not catch has resurfaced: a serial killer who flaunts his sinister intent in front of the Los Angeles Police Department, making it so that no one is safe.

Faith by Matthew LeDrew
Xander's mysterious and troublesome past returns to haunt him on the streets of Los Angeles; a place where even more people can get caught in the crossfire of the games of death and deceit that makes up his life.

Flickers in the Night by Matthew LeDrew
Lisa Rowdan is hunted by her haunting -- and powerful -- ex-boyfriend Ryan through a lonely city street. Can she escape him?
One of over twenty great sprine-tingling short stories!

Family Values by Matthew LeDrew
Xander and his new friends Crowley, Lisa, and Tim investigate a series of kidnappings and murders that stretch back decades, all of which have the same similar twist: victims being found after years of being missing.

The Future

"Remers" by Sarah Thompson
published in *light | dark*.
In the not-too-distant future of the Engen Universe, young athletes are the targets of a scouting program to create the next stage of super soldier with cybernetic enhancements.

about the authors

Ellen Curtis is a writer and web tv personality born and raised in St. Johns, Newfoundland; whose aptitude for the written word began at a young age, when she began writing short stories, poetry, lyrics and novellas.

She was 'discovered' at a Sci-Fi on the Rock writing panel in 2008, and her first collection of stories, *Compendium*, was published just over a year later in October 2009.

Since then she has risen to become one of Engen's lead authors, working on high-profile projects such as the *Infinity* series of adventure novels, as well as continuing her own endeavours.

She has written three novels for the Infinity series, a book of short stories, and is co-editor of the *Sci-Fi from the Rock* series.

In her spare time she enjoys reading, art, music and spending time near the ocean.

Matthew LeDrew studied Journalism at College of the North Atlantic in Stephenville, Newfoundland and has worked with Transcontinental Publishing, as well as the student-youth magazine *The Troubador*.

He has written fifteen other novels for Engen Books: *Black Womb, Transformations in Pain, Smoke and Mirrors, Roulette, Ghosts of the Past* and *Ignorance is Bliss, Becoming, Inner Child, Gang War, Chains, The Long Road, Cinders, Sinister Intent, Infinity*, and *The Tourniquet Reprisal*.

He lives in St. Johns, Newfoundland.